Distracted again, Fleur blinked. "I don't need the extra clothes that have miraculously found their way into my wardrobe."

He shrugged. "I can afford them. And as you're here because I asked you to stay, and you're entering this charade for my sake, it's up to me to bear the cost."

"It's the principle of the thing," she said between her teeth, because she was going to lose this fight. In his world, the amount of money the cosmetics and clothes represented was chicken feed, and he was making sure she understood that.

She felt that gulf between them—huge, uncrossable—and it hurt.

"Besides, you need clothes," he said smoothly, as though paying for her things were a perfectly logical thing to do.

Perhaps in his world it was—but for services rendered, she thought waspishly. A shiver of anticipation ran through her at the thought of what those services might be.

Holding her riotous emotions in check, she said more calmly, "I know you're trying to be helpful, but I feel—" She stopped again, searching for the right word.

"Bought?" Luke supplied helpfully.

Dear Reader,

Harlequin Presents® is all about passion, power, seduction, oodles of wealth and abundant glamour. This is the series of the rich and the superrich. Private jets, luxury cars and international settings that range from the wildly exotic to the bright lights of the big city! We want to whisk you away to the far corners of the globe and allow you to escape and indulge in a unique world of unforgettable men and passionate romances. There is only one Harlequin Presents®, available all month long. And we promise you the world….

As if this weren't enough, there's more! More of what you love…. Two weeks after the Presents® titles hit the shelves, four Presents® EXTRA titles join them! Presents® EXTRA is selected especially for you—your favorite authors and much-loved themes have been handpicked to create exclusive collections for your reading pleasure. Now there's another excuse to indulge! Midmonth, there's always a new collection to treasure—you won't want to miss out.

Harlequin Presents®—still the original and the best!

Best wishes,

The Editors

Robyn Donald
VIRGIN BOUGHT AND PAID FOR

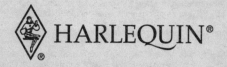

HARLEQUIN®

TORONTO • NEW YORK • LONDON
AMSTERDAM • PARIS • SYDNEY • HAMBURG
STOCKHOLM • ATHENS • TOKYO • MILAN • MADRID
PRAGUE • WARSAW • BUDAPEST • AUCKLAND

Recycling programs
for this product may
not exist in your area.

ISBN-13: 978-0-373-23585-8
ISBN-10:   0-373-23585-2

VIRGIN BOUGHT AND PAID FOR

First North American Publication 2009.

All about the author...
Robyn Donald

Greetings! I'm often asked what made me decide to be a writer of romances. Well, it wasn't so much a decision as an inevitable conclusion. Growing up in a family of readers helped. After anxious calls from neighbors driving our dusty country road, my mother tried to persuade me to wait until I got home before I started reading the current library book, but the lure of those pages was always too strong.

Shortly after I started school, I started whispering stories in the dark to my two sisters. Although most of those tales bore a remarkable resemblance to whatever book I was immersed in, there were times when a new idea would pop into my brain—my first experience of the joy of creativity.

Growing up in New Zealand's subtropical north gave me a taste for romantic landscapes and exotic gardens. But it wasn't until I was in my midtwenties that I read a Harlequin book and realized that the country I love came alive when populated by strong, tough men and spirited women.

By then I was married and a working mother, but into my busy life I crammed hours of writing; my family has always been hugely supportive, even the various dogs that have slept on my feet and demanded that I take them for walks at inconvenient times. I learned my craft in those busy years, and when I finally plucked up enough courage to send off a manuscript, it was accepted. The only thing I can compare that excitement to is the delight of bearing a child.

Since then it's been a roller-coaster ride of fun and hard work and wonderful letters from fans. I see my readers as intelligent women who insist on accurate backgrounds as well as an intriguing love story, so I spend time researching as well as writing.

CHAPTER ONE

A MOVEMENT at the door caught Luke Chapman's eye. So tall he saw above the heads of his guests, he met the newcomer's gaze. Although no one else at the crowded cocktail party would have noticed anything more than the slightest narrowing of Luke's eyes, and a swift, barely perceptible shake of his head, it was enough to make his head of security step back out of the room and wait outside for his employer.

The middle-aged magnate beside Luke lifted his glass. 'Charming little spot you've got here.' He grinned and added slyly, 'Of course you could tuck Fala'isi and its outlying islands in one corner of my ranch in Texas, but we certainly don't have anything like these magnificent mountains. Or your beaches! And this plantation house is something else again.'

Amused, Luke said smoothly, 'We do pride our-selves on our beaches,' before steering the conversation into the prospective ramifications of the collapse of a huge company with worldwide interests.

Ten minutes later, after introducing the Texan to an Australian pastoral tycoon, he made his way across the room, pausing frequently to chat to various guests. Although this sort of social-cum-business occasion wasn't his favourite form of entertaining, in his position as heir to the very small country of Fala'isi—several islands sprinkled across one corner of the Pacific Ocean—they were part of his life. And his decision to hold the party in his parents' house was vindicated; many of the guests had complimented him on the old mansion's beauty and style.

Just outside the door, his security man straightened up.

Luke asked swiftly, 'What's happened?'

'I saw Ms Harrison—Mrs van Helgen—walking along the road. Well, staggering, actually. I stopped to see if she was all right,' Valo told him in a rapid undertone. 'She passed out cold in front of me, so I took her to your place.'

Not a muscle moved in his boss's hard, handsome face. 'How is she?'

'Not too good. When she didn't regain consciousness I called the doctor. She hadn't got there when I left, but I thought you should know.'

'You were right.' Luke looked at his watch. 'I'll be finished in an hour.'

A bright, feminine voice said, 'Luke—so this is where you are!'

The head of security for Chapman Inc watched the younger man turn to the improbably blonde woman in the doorway and smile. It had the usual effect.

His boss's smile worked on everyone—he'd even seen it charm a tantrum-throwing three-year-old into instant submission. As the uncle of the tantrum-thrower, he'd been hugely impressed.

But those who thought his boss just another tycoon's spoilt heir soon learned their mistake. The autocratically chiselled features hid a brain that was cold and incisive and penetrating. Luke Chapman's overwhelming aura cut women off at the knees, yet he was as respected in the arcane world of high finance and business as his father, the legendary Grant Chapman, who held the reins of power in this tiny, hugely wealthy realm.

His head of security looked discreetly away while the woman said something. Luke's voice, deep and deliberate, put her at a slight distance, but not enough to stop her kissing his cheek before she turned back into the room.

He followed her after saying curtly, 'Make sure no one talks.'

She could hear people talking in low, muted tones. She'd been awake before, she knew dimly, but each time she'd immediately slid back into sleep, or maybe it had been unconsciousness?

This time she stayed awake. Over a raging headache, and an even worse thirst, she strained to separate the voices. One was a woman, Australian by her accent, and the other a man with the soft lilt that marked the natives of Fala'isi.

'…dehydrated, and it looks as though she hasn't been eating much, either. She should be all right now that we've got the drip in her, but she'll need care for several days.'

That was the woman. Fleur tried to open her eyes, but the lashes weighted her eyelids.

However, the woman must have seen that abortive flutter. 'She's coming to.'

An arm slipped around her shoulder, lifting her so that someone could nudge a straw between her lips.

'Janna, here's some water. Drink it down—small sips to begin with.'

Janna? Who was Janna? The thought fled as she dragged greedily on the straw, letting the cool water slide down her parched throat, feeling it spread through her body like a benediction.

When the straw was pulled away she croaked a protest, to be told firmly, 'Not too much at first. Just take it slowly. You're on a drip so you'll soon be feeling better.'

There was a stir at the door, a kind of quickening

in the air, as though a presence had arrived. The woman said, 'Ah, Luke, as always your timing is impeccable. She's just woken up.'

Fleur forced her heavy lids up, met a pair of steel-grey eyes, hard and direct and penetrating, in formidably handsome features that seemed vaguely familiar.

His scrutiny was a swift, shocking invasion until he turned away as though dismissing her. 'This isn't Janna.'

He had, she thought in bewilderment, the most wonderful voice she'd ever heard—rich and textured, so potent it stopped the breath in her lungs. She'd heard people speak of dark voices; now she knew what they meant. This one reminded her of bronze, with an underlying note of concentrated authority that should probably warn any woman to watch her step.

She summoned the strength to whisper, 'My name is Fleur.'

Nobody said anything. She closed her eyes and finished wearily, 'Fleur Lyttelton.'

The water had revived her brain enough so that she could think again. Clearly this was a case of mistaken identity, but who was she mistaken for? She could remember walking back along the road to the beach, and the heat. She'd felt sick, and so weary she could hardly put one foot ahead of the other, and then a car had come to a halt beside her...

The odd silence in the room worried her. Frowning, she forced up her lashes to peer at the shuttered face of the man called Luke. He was scrutinising her as though she was some sort of strange being, his cold, metallic gaze slicing through the fragile remnants of her composure like a sword through silk.

'And I'm Luke Chapman,' he said calmly, as though this were an ordinary social occasion.

'How do you do?' she muttered, and thankfully let her lashes cover her eyes again.

Luke felt something stir inside him as he examined her face. Close up she didn't resemble Janna at all, although the hair—long, badly cut, an amazing blaze of primal colour around her white face—was an identical red-gold. However, he suspected Fleur Lyttelton's was natural, unlike Janna's.

Neat features—she'd photograph well—but she didn't have Janna's carefully cultivated beauty. Something stirred deep inside him. There should be a law against mouths like hers—full, subtly sensuous, it was an incitement in itself.

Her lashes drifted upwards again and she fixed him with a wide, slightly vacant stare. The limpid green of the sea at dawn, black-lashed and wide, and with no sign of contact lenses to enhance their colour, they seemed to bore right through him. A tiny frown pleated her narrow dark brows, and she surprised him with a little nod, no more than a queenly inclination of her square chin.

'Thank you,' she said, quite clearly, and slid back into sleep.

The doctor said, 'I'll organise an ambulance, although I don't know where we're going to put her. The hospital's full with this wretched flu epidemic. By the way, the Sulus baby's on the mend.'

'Thank God for that.' Luke's austere expression was transformed by a smile.

The doctor nodded. 'I can put Ms Lyttelton in with the—'

'She can stay here, if that's medically OK?' Luke said, making up his mind instantly.

The doctor's brows shot up. 'Well...no reason why not, I suppose. The drip will need supervision and replenishment, of course, but a nurse can do that, as well as do bloods to check the balance of water and salts in her body. But she's going to be pretty weak for several days, possibly longer.'

Luke nodded, watching the still, uncommunicative face, white against the pillows. In spite of that sensuous mouth, and the tumbled, provocative silk of her red-gold hair, she looked like a woman who'd learned self-discipline in a hard school. He turned to the man who'd picked her up and brought her here. 'I presume she had a bag?'

His head of security indicated a shabby black handbag on the chest at the foot of the bed. 'There.'

'See if she's got any ID, and find out where she's staying, will you?' He looked at the doctor. 'Can you organise a nurse? One who can keep her mouth shut?'

She didn't look surprised. Originally an Australian, she'd spent most of her professional career in Fala'isi, coping with everything the tropics—and the Chapmans—had thrown at her. 'Of course I can. And all my nurses know the value of discretion. One's on leave at the moment, and I happen to know she'd like some extra money. I'll send her over.'

'Thanks.' He left the room, saying once he and the other man were outside, 'Find out about Fleur Lyttelton. Get what information you can from her purse and run a complete check on her.'

When Fleur woke again she could see light glow through her closed eyelids. Instinct told her it was daylight. For a few seconds she lay still, orienting herself. Close by, a dove cooed plaintively, the soft notes backed by the rustle of a breeze in palm tree fronds. A faint fragrance, like vanilla combined with a more exotic scent, transported her back to her mother's kitchen. There that had been the comforting aroma of home and love.

Here it smelt seductive, almost opulent.

Even though her eyelids were too heavy to lift, she knew where she was: in Fala'isi. But instead of the hard ground she'd slept on for the past three nights she was lying on a very comfortable bed. She forced her eyelids up a fraction.

In spite of the spicy perfumes, she expected the usual hospital ward, sparse and institutional; she'd seen enough of them to last a lifetime. But this was a bedroom, modern and enormous, with filmy curtains billowing and stained wooden shutters pushed back against the pale walls.

And she wasn't in a hospital nightgown. Except for a pair of briefs, she was only wearing a tee-shirt. Not one of her own, she realised, looking down at it. Humiliating tears stung her eyes. What was she doing here?

The room's cool, understated simplicity breathed a restrained opulence that intimidated her. A pot of orchids on a long black dressing table made a bold statement against pale walls. The butterfly flowers in shades of scarlet and crimson and gold breathed all the dangerous allure of the tropics. On one wall hung a magnificent panel of *tapa* cloth, its stylised patterns in shades of tan and bronze redolent of the Pacific.

Slightly dizzy, Fleur closed her eyes, but couldn't block out the face that swam into her consciousness—strong, autocratic, totally compelling. Tall and powerfully built, he'd stood by her bed and subjected her to a clinical, unsparing survey.

Was he the owner? The man with the steel-grey eyes and that wonderful voice?

In spite of the sun that spilled through the curtains she shivered, recalling a perfectly moulded mouth that had exuded strength and potency…

Her mind groped for a name, failed, and then caught a fragment of memory. 'Chapman,' he'd said.

Everyone in the Pacific had heard of the family; their status as lords of Fala'isi was the stuff of legends, and the fact that the man who ruled the chain of islands, Grant Chapman, had married a Kiwi meant that the New Zealand women's magazines followed the exploits of their children with great interest, especially the only son and heir apparent.

A sound at the door brought her head around with a jerk. A bad move, she thought dizzily, and sank back onto the pillow as the room wavered hideously in front of her.

A woman in nurse's uniform hurried across to the bed. 'Oh, you're awake at last! How are you feeling this morning?'

'Much better, thank you.' But Fleur's voice was hoarse and she swallowed to ease her dry throat as she closed her eyes again. So she was in hospital— a very up-market one. Perhaps a clinic…

'Here, drink this.'

An arm lifted her while another straw was inserted between her lips. This time she drank without her previous greedy desperation.

'You've been on a drip to get you rehydrated,' the woman told her. 'You certainly look much better than you did last night.'

Just when Fleur had had her fill of water the door opened again and the man walked in, effortlessly dominating his surroundings. It helped, Fleur thought raggedly, that his casual clothes were superbly tailored to fit his big lean frame, but even in a tee-shirt and board shorts he'd give off that same primal, disturbing magnetism.

Luke. His name was Luke, heir to all this beauty and wealth. Fleur stiffened, then set her jaw. Magazine and newspaper photographs hadn't done justice to a face that made him some dark prince of fantasy, its arrogant, uncompromising bone structure honed by tanned skin.

He came across to the bed and smiled at her. It packed a punch, Fleur thought, surprised at the odd little chill that tightened her skin. The swift smile had everything—humour and concern and a smidgeon of sexual interest. It was dangerous.

And so, she thought with a flash of insight, was Luke Chapman.

'You're looking much better,' he said in that deep,

exciting voice. 'Breakfast's on its way. Do you feel well enough to answer a few questions?'

'Yes, of course,' she said weakly. 'Thank you. I don't remember what happened, but…' Her voice trailed away.

He said something in the liquid Polynesian language of the island, and the nurse left the room.

Gaze locked with his, Fleur heard the almost silent closure of the door, leaving her alone with Luke Chapman.

He stood looking down at her, his hooded eyes contrasting with that unsettling, charismatic smile. 'You fainted on the road,' he said in a bland voice, 'just as my driver was passing. He brought you here.'

A frown drew her brows together. 'Why here?' she asked, forcing herself to meet that penetrating stare.

Luke resisted the temptation to shrug. She wasn't going to accept any smooth lies, and although he applauded her caution he wasn't going to tell her that she'd been mistaken for the woman he'd had a brief affair with two years previously.

This morning, a faint wash of pink over her cheeks set off her eyes and mouth. With more colour along those high cheekbones and her stunning hair properly cut she'd be more than appealing, he thought with involuntary masculine appreciation. Rehydration had restored an ethereal bloom to her skin, and her green eyes were huge in their thickets of dark lashes.

'Because the house was closer than the hospital,' he said, and in answer to the question he saw forming on her lips he went on, 'You spent the night here because the hospital is small and needed for real emergencies. We're in the midst of a flu epidemic, and although you probably feel rotten you're not exactly sick, simply dehydrated and exhausted.'

It didn't satisfy her, he could tell. That frown still puckered her brows as she said with automatic politeness, 'Thank you so much, but I have to go.'

'Why?' he asked, intentionally brutal. 'So you can go back to sleeping on the beach? We have laws prohibiting that, you know. How did you get through Immigration without proof of accommodation?'

The delicate colour warmed her face, then faded, leaving her cheekbones standing out too prominently. Not only had she been sleeping rough, he thought with a spurt of irrational anger, but she'd been starving herself as well.

However, she met his eyes steadily. 'I had a holiday cottage booked,' she said. 'But when I arrived there, it appeared that the person who arranged the trip—' she had difficulty saying that '—had made a mistake in the dates. The cottage is occupied.'

'So why not find somewhere else to stay?'

Fleur hated the fact that she blushed so easily—it made people think she was shy and easily manipulated. She wasn't going to tell Luke Chapman that her mother had organised the holiday just before she died. That pain was still too raw.

It was hard to meet those steely eyes, but pride kept her voice level. Ignoring her heated skin, she said, 'I don't have enough money.'

One black brow climbed with calculated affect. 'It didn't occur to you to go to the New Zealand consul here, or ask if someone could help?'

She shook her head, then winced and shut her eyes hastily. It would have been the sensible thing to do, but once she'd discovered that her non-refundable air ticket meant she couldn't get an earlier flight home, she'd thought that in this glorious climate sleeping rough would be fine.

And it had been, until—

Quietly, but with a merciless note in his voice, he stated, 'You had no money in your bag. None at all. And where are your clothes?'

When she didn't answer, he asked again with a little more emphasis, 'Fleur, what happened to your money and your luggage? I assume you had some when you arrived?'

Opening her eyes she said, 'I had—have—a pack. I took it with me when I went to the market to buy some food. I put it down to get my money out of it, and someone came up and offered me a lei made of frangipani flowers—actually slung it around my neck while the stall owner was weighing out the fruit.'

His frown deepened. 'So you bought the pretty lei and when you turned around your pack had gone?'

Her eyes sparked. 'I didn't buy it, but, yes, that's what happened.' When she saw his incredulous look she added in self-defence, 'I only took my eyes off it for a second.'

Straight black brows met over his nose. 'That's all it takes. When did this happen?'

Her mind felt sluggish. She hesitated, trying to count back. 'Three days ago, I think.'

'Did you go to the police?'

'Yes. They were as helpful as they could be, but nobody had seen anything. They did find the pack behind one of the market stalls.'

'Empty?'

'Except for my passport and airline tickets,' she admitted, feeling stupid.

He dismissed them. 'They're not worth anything here. You didn't tell the police your circumstances?'

'No,' she said briefly, irritated by his interrogation into turning her head away.

'You didn't think to contact your credit card company?'

'I don't have a credit card.' Her voice was frosty.

His expression didn't change, and the calm, remorseless interrogation continued. 'Where do you live in New Zealand, Miss Lyttelton?'

'In Waiora, a village on the west coast north of

Auckland,' she said as crisply as she could, trying to sound like her normal competent self. 'Why?'

'I'm just seeing if the facts match your story.'

Fleur closed her lips over the tumultuous words that threatened to break through, and glared at his handsome, implacable face. It took almost all her strength to say evenly, 'I'm telling you the truth.'

'I'm sorry to be so rough on you.' His voice was as controlled as hers, although, she thought in ineffectual anger, with considerably less effort.

'I'm taking that for granted,' she flashed.

At his swift grin her stomach performed an intricate manoeuvre and she felt an alarming shortness of breath.

'So I needn't stress it,' he said. 'You're Fleur Lyttelton of New Zealand, twenty-three years old—and a Leo, I noticed from your birth date.'

His smile might be lethal, but it was his voice that got to her. She had to swallow before she could say curtly, 'I didn't know men were interested in star signs.'

'I have two sisters,' he said with a wry twist to his lips before reverting to an intimidating formality. 'I've put your passport and airline tickets in my safe, where they'll be completely secure. I'm sorry you've had such a rough time. Fala'isi is usually safe, but like any place we have a small number of people who can't be trusted. As it happens, the police tell me they think the pack was probably stolen by another tourist, possibly someone who'd run out of money. They'd stolen the lei from another stall. If it had been a local, someone would have noticed or recognised them.' Without changing his tone he asked, 'Can you sit up without help?'

She stared at him. 'What?'

'You're obviously still thirsty,' he said, and looped an arm around her shoulders, easing her up against the pillows.

So startled she couldn't think, Fleur stiffened while the room lurched again. Close up he was overwhelming, and his touch did strange things to her. Heart beating far too rapidly, she suffered another pillow being stuffed down behind her.

Luke said, 'It's all right. Just blink a couple of times, and then open your eyes slowly.'

His steady tone gave her confidence, although this time it hadn't been movement that caused the room to whirl.

He handed her a glass. 'Keep sipping this. Breakfast will be here shortly, and after that the nurse will help you shower.'

'No—wait.' Under his cold steel-grey scrutiny her confidence dwindled into nothingness. 'I can't stay here,' she said, much less trenchantly than she wanted to.

Black brows drew together in an autocratic frown.

'You're not able to look after yourself. Dehydration can be a killer if it's not monitored, and you're still not out of the woods, so finding other accommodation isn't an option. Neither is sleeping on the beach.'

Angry yet helpless, she met his eyes. The implacable determination she read in them robbed her of strength, so that she said feebly, 'You can't want me to stay here.'

'Don't be foolish.' A note of impatience hardened his voice. 'Believe me, you'll be a lot less trouble if you stay here and are being looked after. We have children so sick they're on oxygen in the hospital. The staff don't need anyone else there unless it's imperative.'

'I—thank you. I think.' She lifted the glass to her lips, using it as a pathetic shield to bolster her shaky defences against his powerful presence.

'You've nothing to thank me for. If you'd done the sensible thing when you realised your plans had gone astray you wouldn't be in this situation. In Fala'isi we don't allow people to starve on our beaches.'

'No doubt because it doesn't look good in the newspapers,' she retorted, and immediately felt ashamed. In his forceful fashion he'd been kind to her.

She expected a cutting reply, but his face didn't give anything away—well, not if she discounted the unwavering aura of authority and assurance that radiated from somewhere deep inside him.

With an undertone of sarcasm, he said, 'If it makes you feel better, yes, that's partly it. We guard the island's reputation zealously, which is why we don't encourage freeloaders and would-be beachcombers. But common humanity is a factor, too. This situation isn't your fault, so the least I can do is help.'

Fleur bit her lip as he walked out of the room, leaving her shaking and wretched. She'd thought she'd cried all her tears before she'd left on this ill-fated holiday, but the let-down from her brief adrenalin rush was churning her emotions into chaos.

CHAPTER TWO

THE return of the nurse with cereal and tropical fruit was a relief.

Settling the tray on Fleur's knees, she said cheerfully, 'Eat it all, the doctor said. Why didn't you ask for food if you couldn't buy it? No islander would have let you go hungry, and there's plenty of food for everyone.'

It was kindly meant, no doubt, but it seemed to Fleur that everyone on Fala'isi felt the need to question her. 'I had enough to eat mostly,' she said defensively.

'Doesn't look like it. What I want to know,' the nurse said with genuine interest, 'is how you managed to hide from everyone that you were sleeping on the beach. The islanders usually know exactly what's happening in their own areas, and you'd have been picked up on any of the resort beaches.'

Fleur flushed. 'I found a tiny bay with only two houses in it—both of them seemed empty holiday houses.'

'About a kilometre away on the road back to town?'

Fleur nodded. 'No one seemed to live there.'

'It's owned by a family who are in Australia for a wedding. They'll be back in a couple of days, so you'd have been found then.'

'I slept under a big tree so even if anyone was on the beach at night they wouldn't see me.' She redirected the conversation. 'This looks delicious, thank you.'

'Coffee or tea?'

The thought of coffee made her stomach roil. 'Tea, please.' And asked impulsively, 'Where am I?' At the nurse's astonished look she added, 'I've seen photos of the Chapman house—a lovely old house. This seems much more modern.'

'Oh, you're thinking of Luke's parents' house, the old mansion.'

Unconsciously Fleur must have hoped that this was a new wing built onto the old plantation-style house, and that any moment Luke's mother might come to see her. The knowledge that she was in Luke's house produced an odd kind of panic, mingled with an even stranger excitement.

Chattily, the nurse went on, 'Luke had this one built a couple of years ago when he came back from overseas and decided he needed his own place. We hoped he might be getting married, but it doesn't look like that's going to happen for a while yet.'

Perhaps realising that this was moving too close to gossip, she smiled and reiterated, 'Eat up everything! Then you can shower. I've brought you a wrap to wear, and a proper nightgown. You need something a bit nicer to wear than Luke's tee-shirt.'

Which brought more heat to Fleur's cheeks. It seemed somehow sinfully decadent to be clad in her reluctant host's shirt.

'Where did you get the wrap and nightgown?' she asked.

'Luke's housekeeper gave me the money, so I suppose it was from Luke.'

Fleur vowed to pay him back, no matter how long it took, but when she thanked him for them he said matter-of-factly, 'Don't worry about that now. Concentrate on eating and sleeping and drinking!'

That day set a pattern for the several that followed, except that she was allowed up for progressively longer periods each day, although both nurse and the doctor when she visited each evening kept a close eye on her welfare.

Luke came in twice a day, bringing with him that instant awareness, a charge of vital energy she'd never experienced before. When he walked through the door she felt invigorated, every sense newly alert, as though previously she'd lived in a kind of stupor.

Apart from those moments, she spent most of her time reading. He had a very good library, she discovered enviously, and once he'd asked her tastes he chose a book for her each day. She also watched videos and the local television station. And she looked wistfully at the wonderful garden she could see from the windows.

She also found that she was too wobbly on her feet to entertain the thought of going out. But the days were long and she disgusted herself by thinking far too much about Luke, and was shocked at the eagerness with which she waited for him to call in night and morning.

The day she was allowed up the nurse arrived with an armful of colour.

'Pareus,' she said. 'In Fiji they call them *lavala-vas*. My daughter sent them along for you.'

'They're beautiful,' Fleur said, 'but I can't wear your daughter's clothes.'

Patiently the older woman told her, 'They're not clothes, they're just a piece of material. She's got dozens. Look, all you do is drape the length right round you and tuck it in. Hold your arms out.'

Feeling both ungrateful and ungracious, after an embarrassed second Fleur obeyed. Deftly the nurse wound the fine cotton around her and showed her the way to tuck it in.

'Won't it come undone?' she asked doubtfully.

'Not unless it gets rough handling,' the nurse said cheerfully. 'Our girls wear them all the time, even swim in them. Now, watch while I show you how to fasten it again.'

Once satisfied that Fleur knew how to do it, she said, 'I've brought some underwear for you, too—Luke told me to buy what you needed. I even found the right bra in one of the shops in town!'

'Thank you,' Fleur said, her pride taking yet another battering.

Under the nurse's supervision she showered, then wrapped herself in the pareu.

'Go and see how you look,' the other woman said, 'while I get you a cup of tea.'

Warily Fleur examined herself in the mirror. The pareu was blissfully cool, and although it showed a lot of pale skin it was modest enough, fastening above any cleavage and falling loosely to knee level.

How would Luke Chapman think she looked in it?

'He probably wouldn't even notice you're wearing something different,' she told her reflection contemptuously. He certainly wouldn't notice that she wasn't wearing a bra beneath it.

The next evening the doctor said, 'Right, you don't need me any more. You're fully recovered from the dehydration, but I'm not too happy about your general health.' She paused as though inviting a confidence.

Fleur said tonelessly, 'My mother died a while ago—I nursed her until she went. I'm fine. Thank you for everything you've done for me.'

Eyes unexpectedly keen, Dr King waved away Fleur's thanks. 'Just doing my job. How long was your mother ill?'

'Five years.'

The doctor nodded. 'And you looked after her all that time?'

'Towards the end she spent quite a bit of time in the hospice,' Fleur told her, keeping her voice level and unemotional.

'I see. Well, when you go home, see your own doctor. You've been under considerable stress, and this last little problem on the island certainly hasn't helped. Talk to him and see what he can do for you.'

'I'm fine,' Fleur said automatically. What could anyone prescribe for grief?

The pleasant Australian said shrewdly, 'Your mother had the right idea—she knew you'd be exhausted, and that you'd need a complete change of circumstances to get the full benefit of any holiday. Dehydration and heat exhaustion certainly played a part in your collapse, but there was more to it than that. Nursing someone you love is exhausting in more ways than the physical. I don't think you should go home until you're fully rested.'

'How long will that be?'

Dr King smiled. 'At least a week,' she said noncommittally.

Fleur said, 'Two days.' When the doctor lifted

her brows she explained, 'I have a non-refundable ticket, and it has to be used then.'

'I see.' The older woman frowned, then said, 'While you're here, stay in the shade and use sunscreen and moisturiser. The tropical sun's hard on skin. And keep drinking at least every half hour.'

She could certainly do that, but now that she was all right, where would she spend the next two days until she could go home?

That night she told Luke what the doctor had said.

'Now you're worrying about it,' he said, and smiled.

In spite of everything, Fleur felt herself surrender to the charm of that smile. An aching warmth seemed to burgeon in her breasts, and to her astonishment she felt the nipples peak into tight, expectant buds.

Hoping desperately it wasn't as obvious to him as it was to her, she said, 'Thank you very much for your kindness. If I can get a lift into town—'

'Don't be silly. It will be dark soon.' He got to his feet and looked down at her, his eyes cool and speculative. 'Have a good night's sleep. Tomorrow you're going to be allowed outside.'

'I'm so looking forward to that,' she said, her fears for the immediate future swamped in the pleasure of being able to do something for herself again.

He didn't come to see her the next morning. Frightened at how much that hurt, she donned a pair of white trousers and a loose cotton shirt—both the right size—spread sunscreen over every inch of exposed skin, and accepted a hat to shade her face.

When she asked who the clothes had belonged to, she was told firmly that they were new. 'Luke bought them,' the nurse finished, as though that was all she needed to know.

It galled Fleur's pride to be a charity case, but again she banished the chagrin by telling herself she'd pay Luke Chapman back somehow, however long it took.

Besides, her spirits were too high now that she was out of the house to brood on something she had no control over. So she reclined in a chair on the private terrace outside her room and read the local newspaper.

Until then she'd only seen the garden from inside. She'd expected tropical gardens to be a riot of colour, and there was indeed a lot of colour there, but it was the form and the myriad shades of the foliage that struck her. As for rioting—well, whoever took care of this garden didn't allow that! For all the bravura effect of huge glossy leaves in every shade of green and gold and bright red, the garden was an exercise in discipline.

Like its owner, she thought, wondering if anything ever managed to disturb Luke Chapman's cool, self-contained confidence.

Making love, perhaps? An odd twist of sensation—heat and hunger combined—coiled up from deep within her.

Embarrassed, she forced herself to concentrate once more on her surroundings. Everything about the place—the choice of plants, the furniture along the terrace, even the tray waiting on the table—was like something out of one of those very expensive magazines that captured the lives of the very rich.

You should be enjoying this, she thought reproachfully. Living in the lap of tropical luxury—it's never going to happen again!

Dutifully Fleur finished the surprisingly hard-hitting pages of local news that included a summary of progress at a conference Luke had presided over—something to do with a Pacific-wide stand on over-fishing. Guiltily she let herself scrutinise a photograph of him. He looked stern and powerful, a truly formidable man—and outrageously handsome.

'High society indeed,' she said aloud, and turned the page to start on the foreign section.

Ignoring the headline that screamed 'MODEL LEAVES HUSBAND OF SIX MONTHS', she tried to read about turmoil in the Common Market, but gave up almost immediately, putting the paper aside.

She lay back in the indecently comfortable lounger and closed her eyes against the sun. Even though she still felt slightly wobbly, it was wonderful to be outside.

However, there was the question of what to do until she left Fala'isi. Overnight she'd managed to ignore the problem, but she had to face it now. She had no money, no clothes and no place to live. And she couldn't stay here.

Almost certainly Luke would be glad to see the back of her; she had no claim on him at all, which meant she had to organise some way out of this impasse.

After fruitless minutes of mulling, she came up with nothing. 'Oh, Mum,' she whispered, fighting back a rush of debilitating tears.

She squared her jaw. No, damn it, she wasn't going to dissolve into a puddle. She owed it to her mother to salvage what she could of the situation.

Opening her eyes, she let the peace sink into her and deliberately stored up memories. Her gaze wandered down a long border where tree ferns canopied a lush planting of peace lilies, their white flowers hovering like doves above glossy leaves. Restful in green and white, the border was finished in the distance by a splash of crimson, bright as a skyrocket against the dark green foliage.

'It's probably just a hibiscus,' she muttered.

Her mother used to pick them and put them on the table, frilly and frivolous with their silken petals and pure, saturated colour, enjoying their fragile temporary beauty.

Fleur's throat tightened. To distract herself, she got up and walked out into the heat to identify that elusive splash of colour.

Halfway there, voices in the distance turned her head. Across the lawn two men were walking along the terrace that surrounded the house. Her unruly heart jumped at the sight of Luke, his tall, lean figure immediately recognisable. She barely noticed the other man, but she felt the impact of Luke's gaze on her, and for some idiotic reason felt that she should have stayed where she was, safe in the little private patio off her room.

Fleur hesitated, but to turn back would be idiotic—and besides, it would make her look suspicious, like someone cas-ing the joint. Setting her teeth, she walked across to the creeper with its bright splash of colour.

It was beautiful, but although she forced herself to examine the flowers, she couldn't enjoy them, and too soon she turned and hurried back to the chair.

The haste was a mistake—one she wouldn't repeat. Head whirling, legs slack and achy, she was sipping water when Luke said from behind her, 'Are you all right?'

Heart jumping, blood pumping through her in a response that came stupidly close to panic, she said thinly, 'I'm fine.'

He stopped in front of her, his too-handsome face

set. 'You're white as a sheet,' he said abruptly. 'Didn't the doctor tell you to take things easily?'

Fleur repressed a gesture of irritation. 'Don't you ever stop asking questions?'

'Once I've got the answers, yes.' He lowered himself into the chair opposite her and surveyed her face with those disconcertingly keen eyes. 'I saw you walking across the lawn. Was it too far?'

'I might have taken it too fast.' She knew she sounded defensive and tried to qualify it with a faint smile. 'I feel like a wimp.'

'Dehydration isn't something to be taken lightly,' he said uncompromisingly. 'And in the tropics it's too easy to forget to drink enough.'

Fleur bit her lip. 'I'm making up for it now. Apparently I have to drink every half-hour.'

'Make sure you do, and if you must move about, take things slowly!'

His tone made her bristle, but she restrained her automatic reaction. He was right, the nurse was right, and she was beholden to them both. And the doctor.

'Yes, sir,' she said, helplessly watching the corners of his mouth lift in that potent smile. Her heart skipped a beat, and she added, 'The funny thing is that I felt pretty good until a few minutes before I—well, fainted so melodramatically in front of your car.'

'It wasn't anything as easily dealt with as a faint. You collapsed,' he said brutally.

'Yes, well, I'm better now,' she said. She sat up straight and squared her shoulders, making her voice brisk and impersonal. 'Thank you so much for everything you've done. I'll find some other accommodation—'

'Don't be silly,' he drawled, thick lashes shading his eyes. 'I've checked, and the cottage is booked solid for another month. You have no money, and as Dr King wants you to be where someone can keep an eye on you, I told her you'd stay here as my guest until you return to New Zealand.'

'No!'

'You needn't look at me as though I've made you an indecent proposition,' he drawled, an amused glint in his eyes making her squirm. 'It's by far the best way to handle the situation.'

Fugitive colour burned across her skin. 'I couldn't possibly impose on you,' she said stiffly.

'You're not going back to sleeping on the beach,' he said with ruthless frankness. 'In fact, you're not going anywhere for a while. On the doctor's recommendation I've cancelled your return ticket.'

Eyes flashing, Fleur sat up straight. 'You—she—had no right to do that!' she spluttered, barely able to articulate.

'Dr King said that not only were you suffering from dehydration, but that you're exhausted and run-down and very close, she suspects, to burning out. She doesn't want to see you travel for at least a week, and possibly a fortnight.'

'A fortnight!' Her brain raced frantically, but he looked so arrogantly confident she was reduced to a kind of mental stammering, and could only stare impotently at him.

'Do you have a home to go to in New Zealand?'

Mutely, Fleur glared at him. 'I have a room in a boarding house,' she said. A small, hot room.

Luke's brow lifted in ironic surprise. 'So exactly what were you planning to do once you got back to New Zealand?'

She'd planned to take up a temporary job in the local supermarket and regroup, find some direction to her life.

Ruthlessly Luke pressed home his advantage. 'Dr King doesn't feel happy about your going back unless you have support waiting for you in New Zealand. Do you?'

Fleur wouldn't lie, so she folded her lips and stared silently at him.

'No friends to make sure you're all right?'

No one close, but she wasn't going to tell him that, either.

He said sardonically, 'Of course I can't keep you here if you don't want to stay, so I'll organise a private room for you in the hospital until the doctor says you're fit to travel. You can go home in the family's private jet—'

'No, don't be silly!' she spluttered, pressing her palms to her hot cheeks. 'I don't want a room in the hospital, not when every one is needed for sick people. It never occurred to me that you even had a private jet!'

'I'm merely pointing out your options.'

Fleur took her hands away from her face and asked desperately, 'Surely there's somewhere else I can stay?'

'Not in your present state.' He waited, then said, 'Look, you won't be imposing on me at all—as you've probably gathered, my staff do the actual work around here. If you stay here both the doctor and I will be reassured that you're OK, and that you're eating and drinking properly.'

He made it sound so reasonable, she thought with difficulty. 'I don't know…'

'And when you're feeling up to par I'll lend you enough money to see out your holiday—'

'No,' she interrupted, the heat fading from her skin. Head held high, she said proudly, 'I can't afford to repay you.'

Long black lashes half hid his eyes, but couldn't mask the penetrating quality of his scrutiny. 'Do you want to tell me about it?'

'No,' she said, more calmly. There was no way out; she'd have to accept. 'Now that you've cancelled my flight I have no alternative but to accept your offer. I'll try not to get in your way at all, and if there's anything I can do to repay you, I will.'

It sounded false even as she said it—because what could she do, penniless as she was, to repay him? But her pride demanded she make the offer.

He didn't answer, and the silence stretched beyond the normal length. Startled, she looked up. He was watching her, grey eyes like polished steel, intent and probing.

Something hot and reckless that had been smouldering deep inside her burst into flame, burning into the barriers she'd erected against him. And then she realised what she'd said.

Appalled, she thought, Surely he doesn't think—? Surely he can't—?

Oh, why did she have to blush every time she got embarrassed?

She stumbled into speech. 'I don't mean—that is, I'm not offering—'

'Yourself?' The word hung in the air between them. Fleur crimsoned. 'Yes. I mean, no, I'm not…'

He suddenly laughed. 'I'm sorry,' he said, and that strange intensity vanished. 'I was teasing. It's probably just as well you didn't have brothers— they'd have made your life a misery.'

'I'd have learned how to deal with them,' she returned tartly, feeling a total fool.

He grinned. 'Probably.' He glanced across the lawn, and said, 'Ah, here's Susi with lunch. I suggest we discuss the state of the world while we eat and drink, and then I think you probably should go back inside. Dr King was very firm about not too much exercise and as little exposure to the sun as possible.'

Susi was a large, comfortable-looking woman who looked at her closely when Luke introduced her as the housekeeper. Something about her gaze set Fleur's teeth on edge, until the big woman relaxed into smiles and offered her hand in a hearty shake.

'On Fala'isi we introduce staff,' Luke said when she'd left them. 'Here everyone is related, and they can usually tell you to an exact degree the degree of relationship.'

'That must be lovely,' she said quietly.

'You sound as though you don't have much close family.'

She moved uncomfortably. 'A father in Australia,' she admitted. 'And at least one half-sibling, I've been told. No one else.'

The corners of his beautifully chiselled mouth lifted in a wry smile. "The thing about relatives is that they have a vested interest in every aspect of your life and an opinion on everything you do.'

Fleur remembered the nurse's comment that they'd thought his new house meant a marriage. 'I suppose there are disadvantages to everything, but that seems a minor one compared to the advantages. How did everyone get to be related?'

He told her of the ancestor who'd landed on Fala'isi only to find it almost depopulated by diseases brought by Europeans. His description of that first wild seafarer's forced marriage to the only surviving child of the paramount chief's family fascinated her. The story—sometimes brutal, sometimes unexpectedly lightened by flashes of compassion and kindness—was utterly compelling.

Finally he said, 'I have to go out in a few minutes, but we'll meet for a drink before dinner.'

He got to his feet, and once again Fleur realised how tall he was—a naturally dominant man, lean and big, who moved with the powerful litheness of a predator at the top of the food chain.

She took a deep breath and stood up, too, holding herself desperately erect, but when she took her first step she managed to sabotage herself by stumbling against the leg of her chair.

Like the predator she'd likened him to, he moved fast, his hand fastening onto her arm and holding her upright. His closeness stirred her physically and in other, more subtle ways—she wanted to lean against him, to absorb some of that strength and power, to let him—

Alarm bells clanging in her mind, she thought desperately, *Get out of here! Now!*

She flinched and tried to step free, making a soft sound of dismay when she found that her legs refused to obey her brain's command.

'I think probably the best way to do this is for me to carry you,' Luke said judicially, and, ignoring her shocked objection, he picked her up as effortlessly as if she'd been a child and strode into her bedroom.

Fleur wanted to command him to put her down, but her bones were too heavy and she felt waves of tiredness wash over her. For the first time since her father had left her and her mother, she felt a sense of utter security. She might not approve of Luke Chapman's ruthlessness, but she felt utterly safe in his arms, her fuzzy brain accepting him as though it had been waiting for him for years.

'I'm fine,' she blurted.

He didn't put her down until they reached the bed. 'Rest until later in the afternoon,' he commanded, looking down at her with complete confidence that she'd do exactly as he ordered. 'And in case you feel like doing something stupid—walking out, for instance—the staff know that you're staying. You wouldn't get far.'

Incredulously, Fleur lifted her head off the pillows to meet his uncompromising eyes. 'I hope you're not insinuating that I'm a prisoner here.'

'I'm not insinuating anything,' he returned, assessing her with an enigmatic gaze. 'I'm telling you that the staff know that you're not fit to leave, so they won't let you. Only a Leo would call that being taken prisoner.'

She said irritably, 'I'll bet you're a Scorpio.'

'You're an astrologer?' he asked with a hint of cynicism.

'No, but I know a Scorpio when I meet one. You all have that innate arrogance.'

He laughed. 'I draw the line at you telling me that I share some of my genetic traits with one-twelfth of the population. My mother says it's a Chapman characteristic.'

'She should know,' Fleur said crisply.

Luke found himself admiring her. According to the information Valo had pulled together she was penniless after her mother's long illness, her future without prospects, yet although she wasn't yet up to par she was full of fight. Her cool, still pride, oddly at variance with that mane of red-gold hair, both amused and touched him.

'Are your parents here?' she asked remotely.

He heard the rapid chill in the voice that should be slow and warm, with its lazy, sensuous undertone that made him think of cool sheets on a hot summer night...

'No,' he said, irritated by the reaction from a part

of his body that had no right to be responding. 'They're holidaying in the Caribbean. If they were here, you'd have been staying with them.'

Fleur felt as though she'd been put firmly in her place. A nuisance.

CHAPTER THREE

ONCE he'd gone Fleur was sure her roiling mass of emotions would prevent any rest, but now she was on that supremely comfortable bed sleep claimed her with voracious speed.

She woke to the seductive cooing of doves, their tranquil notes floating on the drowsy air. Tropical scents—sweet, heavy, sharpened with the all-pervading perfume of vanilla—summoned a long, slow sigh to her lips, followed by a wavering smile. Not since before her mother's condition had rapidly worsened a year ago had she slept like that.

How strange, she thought, listening to the muted roar of the waves on the reef. In spite of everything—her prickly reaction to her arrogant host, her experience of living rough—she could sleep as soundly as though she'd reverted back to her childhood, when her world had been bright and shining and seamless.

If this was the fabled spell of the Pacific, she was hooked.

Yawning, and feeling much more human, she got up and showered in the white-tiled bathroom with its wooden shutters, sprays of orchids and air of restrained opulence.

Now, she thought, what on earth am I going to wear if I have to stay here for another week?

Even if by some miracle her pack turned up with its contents intact, she had nothing suitable. She hadn't been able to afford new clothes for this ill-fated holiday. Her sundresses, shorts and the couple of tops were all several years old, and fitted a more rounded woman than the one who'd cared for her mother these past years.

A soft tap at her door swivelled her around.

But of course Luke Chapman wasn't there. Instead, Susi, in a pareu of bold scarlet and dark blue, said, 'Luke would like it if he could join you on the terrace outside in half an hour, miss. I'll collect you then.'

And that, Fleur decided as she watched the door close, was definitely an order.

So why was her heart skipping unevenly and a slow, sensu-ous warmth stealing through her veins like a drug?

Glowering at her reflection, Fleur wished she'd surrendered to the seduction of some sexy little silk tee-shirts she'd seen in the market. But, cheap as they were, they'd still been too expensive for her.

And even if she had bought one, it would have been stolen like the rest of her gear.

Besides, tee-shirts were not for her. Her mother used to say she had an Edwardian hourglass figure, a small waist emphasised by maternal hips and breasts that were slightly too ample for the rest of her. Tee-shirts clung and made her look conspicuous.

At least the colour suited her. Whoever had chosen the outfit had known that camel silk would go with her bright hair and pale skin. After a last defiant look at her neat, uninteresting reflection, she tucked a stray strand of hair back into place just as the housekeeper tapped at the door.

However, it was Luke who stood in the corridor outside, not Susi. 'If I give you an arm, do you think you could make the few yards to another terrace?' he asked, his expression noncommittal.

Fleur's heart gave another of those peculiar jumps in her chest. 'Of course,' she said brightly, and fixed her eyes on the magnificent portrait at the end of the hallway—an elegant woman of the thirties.

'My great-grandmother,' he said, following her gaze. 'She was French.'

No wonder she radiated that sleek, effortless chic. 'She looks fascinating.'

'She was.' His tone was affectionately reminiscent.

There were resemblances—the midnight hair, and possibly his brilliant clothes sense. Luke's shirt matched his steel-grey eyes, and his trousers had been tailored to reveal his long, powerful legs. But where had his boldly chiselled face come from, underpinned by the magnificent bone structure that gave him such authority and that intimidating air of mastery and force? Add that to a lithely powerful body, and you had the sort of man women dreamed of.

So the rapid thud of her heartbeat in her ears was quite understandable, as was the heat that crept into her skin when he gave her a lazy smile after he'd tucked her into a chair at their destination, a long terrace with a sunset view over the lagoon.

'You look infinitely more yourself,' he said gravely.

'I must have looked pretty dreadful before.' Her green glance gleamed in challenge.

'Exhaustion has that effect on people,' he agreed. 'According to Dr King, alcohol would be all right if suitably diluted. I can offer you a very weak gin and tonic, if you'd like that.'

'Could I just have something nonalcoholic and not too sweet? Fruit juice will be fine.'

'We have plenty of fruit juice.' He poured her a glass.

Fleur sipped it gratefully. 'It's delicious,' she said with a smile. 'Perfect.'

'I'm glad you like it—it's Susi's secret recipe. Pineapple, of course, and papaya and mango, and some spices she refuses to divulge.'

'Vanilla, perhaps?' When he looked quizzically at her she said, 'The whole house is delicately scented with it.'

'The whole island,' he corrected. 'We grow it for export. It's an orchid, and we're lucky to have just the right conditions for it to flourish.'

A dove flew down onto the lawn a few feet away and pecked, the contrast of its white plumage and the vivid coarse green grass almost startling.

Fleur let out a long, soft sigh. 'This is so beautiful,' she said quietly, watching the sun dip towards the horizon.

While the great, flaming disc edged its way into the sea, Luke told her about the green flash that was part of the folklore of the tropics.

'So it's only ever seen at sunset?' she marvelled.

'Even then conditions have to be absolutely right. No one seems to know what causes it.'

'It sounds—amazing,' she said quietly. 'Have you seen it?'

'A couple of times.'

The swift tropical dusk was falling as darkness swept in from the east. Luke got to his feet and lit candles at the table; their soft, romantic light flickered a little in the breeze that ruffled across Fleur's acutely sensitised skin. The small lights settled, washing gold over the dark planes of his face.

A stab of some unknown sensation took Fleur by

surprise. She knew she was attracted to him, but attraction didn't describe this fierce hunger that seemed to blast out of nowhere and take her over.

Fortunately he didn't notice. Over the drink they talked of nothing much, the sort of light conversation that sophisticated people like Luke Chapman did so well. Fleur was grateful to him for his tact; the past year had been spent almost entirely in conversation with medical personnel, and she'd nearly forgotten how to do idle conversation. He made it easy for her, and although over dinner she realised he was learning a lot about her, she responded easily.

Until she found herself talking about her mother.

Then her voice faltered; tears ached behind her eyes and she took refuge in the glass of water he'd poured for her.

'I'm sorry,' Luke said quietly.

'It's all right.' She set the glass down and fought for composure. He didn't seem embarrassed, and he didn't try to hurry her up.

Eventually she said in a brittle voice, 'It's just that—she died about six weeks ago, after spending five years fighting a progressive illness. She organised the holiday and paid for it before she died— she used to worry about me not having any fun.' Her throat thickened. 'She'd have been h-horribly upset if she'd known that the travel agency had got the dates wrong.'

'She'd probably have been more horrified if she'd known you were going to tough it out by sleeping on the beach,' he said grimly.

She flashed him an indignant glance. 'I didn't sleep on the beach. I had a comfortable nest under some bushes nearby, and I felt perfectly safe.'

'You were lucky. We work damned hard to keep the island free of crime, but even so, we can't vet every tourist who comes in. Or, unfortunately, all of the islanders. Once you'd lost your money you should have realised you were in an untenable position. People can survive starvation for much longer than they realise, but it was stupid to emulate them when there was no need. Any islander would have given you food.'

'I was managing. I ate fruit from the trees on the side of the road. I only fainted—'

'Collapsed,' he interjected uncompromisingly.

'I only *fainted,*' she repeated with more emphasis, 'because I'd walked a long way in the heat and stupidly I'd forgotten to fill my water bottle.' And then she remembered something that had completely skipped her mind. 'Who is Janna?'

His brows drew together. The frown lasted only a second, and his voice was easy and pleasant when he answered, 'She's a friend of mine. Why?'

'When I woke I thought you called me Janna. No, someone else did.' She searched her brain, thinking out loud. 'You said, "This is not Janna." But that's who your man thought I was, and that's the reason he brought me here. I'd forgotten until now.'

'He brought you here because it's a half-hour drive to the hospital and he was worried,' Luke said evenly. 'I wasn't here, but when you didn't regain consciousness the staff decided to call the doctor. By the time I got home she'd checked you over and fixed up the drip. If you hadn't collapsed in front of the car you could well have become dangerously ill—most people don't realise how much water you need to drink in the tropics.'

Soberly she said, 'I realise now, believe me. It's not an experience I want to repeat.' She looked at him. 'I don't think I've ever thanked you for taking me in. I'm truly grateful—'

'It's not necessary,' he interrupted curtly, getting to his feet. 'And you're looking smoky around the eyes, so I suggest it's time for you to go to bed.'

Of course she acquiesced, and it wasn't until just before tiredness overwhelmed her that she realised he'd told her nothing about the mysterious Janna, the woman she apparently resembled closely enough for almost everyone at the house to have believed that was who she was. Except for Luke, who'd known instantly that she wasn't.

His lover?

Almost certainly, she thought as she slid into

sleep. That air of authority was underpinned by a compelling sexuality. Somehow, without him being at all overt, any woman meeting him knew that he'd be a superb lover…

Luke put down the receiver and swore luridly in a mixture of Polynesian and English. Then he stood and walked across to the window and stared out into the darkness, his mind racing furiously.

Five minutes later he picked up the telephone again. His chief of security answered; from the sounds in the background it was obvious he was socialising.

'Sorry to interrupt,' Luke said abruptly. 'I've just heard from a contact in Germany that Eric van Helgen's disappeared. And yesterday morning I was interviewed by a Common Market journalist, who happened to leave the house at the same time that Ms Lyttelton walked across the lawn in full sight, her hair very much in evidence.'

After a tense silence, the other man said, 'So Ms van Helgen is in danger.'

'Possibly. Though I can think of reasons for his secrecy—their break-up has already been splashed through the world's papers, and if he wants to reconcile with Janna the last thing he needs is paparazzi dogging his every footstep.'

'What do you think?'

Luke said slowly, 'I don't know.' Janna was spoilt, and she'd been angling for his sympathy. Her story of violence and fear had sounded genuine enough, but Luke had caught her out in previous exaggerations. 'There's the fact that the research you did on him didn't back her story at all.'

'Not a shred of evidence.'

'But we can't ignore her completely. Alert the airport and tell them you want to know if he's booked on a flight here. You've got photographs of him, haven't you?'

'Yes. I'll make sure the immigration officials understand that they need to be on the alert. What do you want to do if he turns up?'

'Let me know first, and put your best man onto tailing him,' Luke said. 'See what he does.'

'And if he comes with false papers?'

'If he tries that, he probably assumes that Fala'isi is some tropical backwater where money will get you anything, so he's not going to be too careful. Let him think he's got away with it, but again, watch him.'

'Fortunately we've got the perfect decoy to convince him that he's made a huge mistake by coming here.'

Luke thought of the woman who'd been resident in his house for the past few days. He said curtly, 'Hell, no. Ms Lyttelton has nothing to do with this mess. Keep looking into his background. Work your links and connections—trawl for anything at all that might back up Janna's allegations. If you find any dirt at all, or if van Helgen arrives, we'll get both Janna and Ms Lyttelton off the island as quickly and inconspicuously as we can. If his wife's story is true he's a very dangerous man.'

'What do you think?'

'I think she made the whole thing up.' He paused, then added fairly, 'No, it's more likely she's embroidered a quarrel they had and has now convinced herself that her tale is true.'

His man's frown showed up his voice. 'So you just want him watched?'

'For the time being. Oh, and get your wife to bring out a selection of clothes for Ms Lyttelton tomorrow, will you? She needs everything, so a complete new wardrobe is in order.' He gave the sizes.

Fleur turned away from the mirror with a grimace. During these past few days she'd spent entirely too much time staring at her reflection. But this morning before Luke left the house he'd sent along a note with the housekeeper asking her to join him on the terrace for lunch, and as Susi had whisked away the shirt and trousers she'd worn before, 'For cleaning, miss,' Fleur was forced to wear a pareu.

It showed too much of her skin, she thought critically, and the colours—a mixture of orange-red and

periwinkle-blue with a light, clear bold purple—
were shockingly flamboyant, but somehow they
seemed to bring colour and life to her face, while
not clashing with her vivid hair. Perhaps the earthy
tans and greens she'd always worn had been wrong
for her pale colouring.

Or perhaps it was the spell of the tropics.

When Luke greeted her, she saw his gaze go from
her face to her breasts in one swift reconnaissance.
He didn't ogle, but she had no doubt that he
approved of her change of clothes. Heat fountained
up from some previously inviolable place in her
body, and she felt an odd tightening in her breasts.

Holding onto her fragile composure with every
bit of her pride, she said as she slipped into the
chair, 'Susi persuaded me to wear this. I hadn't
realised how cool they were.'

Yes, that was fine; her voice was steady, her tone
light—only the faint pinkness of her skin gave her
away. Nothing less than a shroud would cover that,
she thought despondently, wishing she hadn't inherited her mother's tendency to blushes.

Her senses seemed supercharged, so that she was
vibrantly conscious of the man who seated himself
opposite her and acutely aware of the air caressing
her skin, and the warmth of the sun, and the delicious scent of some flower.

Rest and good food and rehydration had certainly

made a difference, she told herself tartly. She felt more alive than she had for years.

'Would you like coffee?' he asked. And when she accepted he said, 'Could you pour for me, please? Black.'

'Of course,' she said brightly. 'Scorpios always have black coffee. It goes with the sign.'

Luke watched her slim, elegant hands as she poured the coffee. They did odd things to him, summoning reckless images that had no place at the lunch table—images of them stroking slowly over his skin.

He'd spent half his life being chased by women and understood them well. He took it for granted that most were far more attracted to his money than to him, but he'd have been an idiot not to know that the genes responsible for his face and body had their own appeal.

So he recognised the signs of physical response in Fleur, though she certainly wasn't giving him any obvious signals. A pretence of aloofness to pique his interest? He didn't think so, but his attention was certainly aroused. Apart from his sympathy for what had to have been a traumatic experience, he wanted to know more about her.

He said coolly, 'I have to apologise for being remiss—it's been a busy few days, but now the conference is over things will be back to normal. Or as normal as it ever gets here. And, as you can't continue walking around in borrowed pareus, I've organised a local boutique owner to bring a selection of clothes here this afternoon. Choose what you want.'

Fleur wasn't sure she'd heard correctly. Outrage warring with a demoralising pleasure, she looked up and met hooded iron-grey eyes. 'You didn't have to do that,' she said stiffly. 'I can organise my own wardrobe.'

'Relax, I'm not casting aspersions on either your clothes or your taste,' he said with infuriating calmness, adding to her anger by finishing, 'And how are you going to organise a wardrobe without money?'

He looked amused, but Fleur sensed a hard will behind the coolly confident exterior.

Well, her mother had always said she was stubborn. 'If you lend me a small amount of money I can get a selection of sarongs from the market—they don't cost much and they're all I need. Then I can return the ones I've been wearing to the nurse's daughter.'

'Don't worry about the cost—you must know that I have more money than I can cope with. Think of it as redressing the balance a bit.'

Green fire glittered in her eyes. 'Redressing what balance? I don't want to accept anything more from you—you've already been far too good to me. In fact, I feel well enough to go home now.'

'Did Dr King say so?'

She hesitated. 'No,' she admitted reluctantly, after

a glance at Luke told her that he knew exactly what the doctor had told her. 'Clearly she has no hesitation in breaking patient confidentiality.'

Luke's shoulders lifted in a shrug that reminded her of his French great-grandmother. 'I knew most of it, and guessed the rest,' he drawled. 'And if staying here galls you so much, you can earn your keep.'

She froze. 'How?' The word came more sharply than she'd intended.

'Not the way you're thinking,' he told her with a hint of hauteur. 'I've never had to pay for sex, and I don't intend to start now.'

Fleur had always thought that the desire for the ground to swallow some embarrassed soul was weird, one that made her shudder. Now she understood the power of total humiliation. If the ground had cracked open in front of her she'd have leapt into the hole without hesitation.

Scarlet-faced, she said, 'I didn't think of anything like that until you…made it obvious what you thought I meant.' Before she got too hopelessly tangled, she took a deep breath, then ploughed valiantly on. 'I understand that it wasn't what you meant, but I'm afraid I don't have any skills to pay for my board.'

'Let's get one thing perfectly clear,' he said, his gaze metallic. 'I don't expect you to pay for anything. What I meant by my offhand comment was that I find myself in somewhat of a bind, and if you're agreeable, you can help me.'

'I'd like to,' she said quietly. 'You've been very kind to me and I'm not ungrateful.'

'I don't want your gratitude,' he said, his aloofness setting a boundary between them. 'The situation I'm in is an unusual one. An old friend of my father's is arriving to stay soon, and bringing his granddaughter with him to a charity affair we're all attending. Gabrielle is young, very pretty, and I like her, but she's suffering a massive crush on me, and it's becoming embarrassing.'

'They usually are—to both the crusher and the crushee,' Fleur said tartly. And she didn't believe for a second that this was an unusual situation for him.

'This is sliding over the edge into something that comes just a bit close to stalking for my liking. I've just read an interview she gave to a fashion magazine. She implied that she and I are engaged, and that I'm just waiting for her to grow up.'

Rapidly revising her impression of a high school Gabrielle, Fleur asked, 'How old is she?'

'Nineteen. She's a model.'

'I'm surprised. I'd have thought you'd be able to deal with a situation like this.'

'Normally I would.' His voice hardened. 'But her grandfather is old, and it would hurt him if my lawyers sent her a letter telling her to desist, or if I contacted the press with a denial. And I like the girl—I don't want to humiliate her.'

'Somebody must have given her the idea that you were in love with her.'

He paused. 'Not I.'

Fleur was inclined to believe him. After all, with all the women he could pick and choose from, it seemed unlikely that he'd choose one so young. 'So how do you think I can help?'

He looked enigmatically at her. 'You've been staying here for several days, and it might reinforce that I am not interested in her as wife material if we convince her that we're lovers.'

'Lovers?' Her voice hit a high, shocked note.

He lifted her hand from the table and got to his feet, bringing her with him. 'Lovers,' he repeated calmly, a cynical smile tilting the corners of his mouth. 'As in sharing a bed.'

'As in being your mistress?' Her heart was thumping so loudly she could barely hear her words, and she couldn't tear her eyes away from his, gunmetal grey and direct, yet heated in some mysterious way.

'Mistress? That's a very old-fashioned word,' he said with an odd inflexion. Still holding her hand, he lifted his other one to trace the outline of her lips.

His touch was pure fire, lightning in her blood, a fever on her skin.

'No,' he said deeply. 'Apart from that erotic

mouth, you're not mistress material. In fact, Gabrielle is light years ahead of you in sophistication. A mistress she could deal with. I want her to believe that we're in love, that this is serious.'

One knowledgeable finger smoothed along one cheekbone. Trying hard to muster her thoughts into some coherent form, she muttered, 'If she's so sophisticated she'll know…she'll know…'

'What will she know?' His voice was amused, and when she lifted her lashes she could see that he was watching her mouth with narrowed, intent eyes.

An electric charge shot through her, setting every cell humming in dangerous intoxication. 'That… that I'm not the right sort of person for you.'

It was so difficult to articulate her tumbling thoughts. She tried to ignore the compelling fascination of his dark voice, that hypnotic glint in his eyes and the slow, sensuous caress across her skin, the touch she felt right down to her innermost core.

Rallying herself, she said, 'I mean, I'm not the sort of person you'd be attracted to. I blush all the time. It's my skin—it's the sort that shows colour—'

She was babbling and she cut back the words, afraid that she was making a total fool of herself. Pull away, she commanded her body. Step back. He's only holding one hand—he'll let you go…

His gaze darkened. 'Ah, but you're wrong. I find you very attractive—surely you've realised? Your skin is like silk, and the blushes you find so dismaying are charming.'

He released her hand, but before she could take the opportunity to leap backwards he cupped her face with both hands and smiled at her.

Even in her dazzled state, Fleur was aware that he was consciously using his charm and compelling male presence to persuade her. She should be angry—but when he smiled at her she felt its erotic impact zing like lightning through her body.

However, he dropped his hands and took the step backwards himself, a touch of colour along his cheekbones reassuring her that he hadn't been entirely unaware of her as a woman, even if it had been in the most basic way.

He said, 'Trust me, if you agree, they will believe that we are in love. The men in my family marry for love. And this will be the least painful way—and probably the only one they'd accept—for Gabrielle to find out that her hopes and dreams are nothing more than fairy gold.'

'Will she be upset?'

Again his broad shoulders lifted. 'Almost certainly a little,' he conceded. 'But surely it's better that than to waste several years believing she's in love with me and that we're meant for each other, or to suffer public humiliation when I make it obvious that I'm not interested in her as a wife.'

'I suppose so.' Although every instinct of self-preservation was howling a warning, Fleur said, 'Very well, I'll do it.'

It would be one way of repaying him for some of his consideration. And she'd be quite safe, because you couldn't fall in love so quickly. You had to know someone to love them, and even then, she thought with a shiver of remembrance, love was often based on illusion. She'd live a fantasy life for a short time and then she'd go back to her everyday life without a regret.

Luke didn't overwhelm her with effusive thanks. His smile was ironic, a little twisted. 'Thank you. So treat the clothes as a necessary part of your role. And to establish that, tonight I'm hosting a dinner party for twenty. Don't look so alarmed, I won't expect you to be the hostess—'

'Which is just as well, because I've never hosted a dinner party in my life,' she said, terrified at the thought of pretending to be Luke's lover in front of his friends. 'Do I have to be there? We don't have to fool *them*—I can have dinner in my room.'

'Like a Victorian governess? Your presence here has been noticed,' he said, adding with crisp ruthlessness, 'Of course if anyone asks me where you are I can tell your sad little story.'

She drew in a hiss of breath between her teeth. 'You fight dirty,' she said unsteadily. 'I'll be totally out of my depth and you know it. I'm sure you're trying to be kind, but—'

Luke gave a short bark of laughter. 'I'm not, and *you* know that. I dislike seeing anyone cut off their nose to spite their face—it's always seemed a pastime singularly lacking in sense or entertainment value. You don't need to come to the dinner party but I think you'd enjoy it, just as I'm sure you'll enjoy the day we plan to spend out on the lagoon tomorrow.'

She flushed. 'I'm being ungrateful, aren't I?'

Luke had always chosen sophisticated lovers, sure of themselves and their own attractions, yet he found her pride and her embarrassment endearing. She was fresh and charming and her mouth promised erotic delights untold, but everything about her warned him that she was totally lacking in the worldliness he'd always sought in his women.

Coolly he said, 'I told you before, I don't want gratitude. And if you're wondering whether I'd expect you to indulge in overt displays of affection you needn't worry—I'm not so crass. I merely thought that tonight would be a test run, and that you might be able to think yourself into the part easier if Gabrielle and her grandfather were not here.'

CHAPTER FOUR

FLEUR looked up into Luke's tough, formidable face. What am I *doing?* she thought in panic.

But she said, 'Very well, I'll come. I just hope nothing goes wrong.'

'Nothing can,' he said with supreme self-confidence, and glanced at the watch on one lean tanned wrist. 'Can you be ready to have a look at some clothes in half an hour or so?'

'I—yes.' Of course she could be ready! She had nothing else to do. But she was hugely reluctant.

She spent most of that half-hour wondering why on earth she'd agreed to this crazy idea. A sense of obligation carried to extremes, she decided, feeling another flick of panic. Yet Luke had taken her in and cared for her, and although he hadn't done any of the actual work, he'd assumed responsibility for her when she was incapable.

The least she could do was help him out in turn. Susi came to escort her to one of the other bedrooms. A selection of clothing was already waiting on racks, along with a woman dressed in a very up-market version of a pareu.

And Luke.

Did he expect her to parade in front of him like a model? Her whole being cringed at the prospect. She opened her mouth to ask him what he was doing there, only to bite back the words when she met his level, intimidating gaze.

He said easily, 'Thank you, Susi.' He waited for the housekeeper to leave before introducing her to the other woman, then said, 'I'll leave you to try the clothes on.'

Relieved, Fleur nodded.

Once he'd gone the boutique owner surveyed her with professional expertise. 'He had the size right. And the colours—clear and warm to complement your astonishing skin and hair. He's got a good eye, that boy.'

'Boy?'

The older woman grinned. 'I've known him since he was running around in a faded old *lavalava* with the other children. He might be almost thirty, but to me he'll always be a wild kid. Now, let's see what you like most.'

Given her head, Fleur would have chosen the muted colours she'd always worn, but as she'd tried on the clothes in crisp, clear hues, she realised that Luke had been right; the warm, peachy shades brought her skin and eyes alive, and the crisp peridot-greens turned her eyes into jewels.

Fleur and the saleswoman had a slight, polite tussle over the number of clothes to be purchased. 'This is enough,' Fleur said firmly, indicating the small pile she'd settled on.

However much they suited her, she wouldn't need more than a fraction of the outfits carefully hung on a separate rack. There were no prices anywhere, but she recognised some labels, and the finishing and materials told her they didn't come from the cheap range.

And then there were the extras—the underclothes and shoes and hats—things she'd only ever wear once or twice.

The older woman said doubtfully, 'You'll need more than that. The tropics are pretty tough on clothes.'

'I can manage,' Fleur said firmly.

The woman nodded. 'OK, your decision. Now, can I make a suggestion? Your hair is glorious, but the style isn't doing it justice. I have a friend who cuts like a genius, and she could come and do it for you now if you want her to. As a favour to Luke.'

Tactfully phrased, but the woman had meant, *Your hair looks awful.*

Most of the time Fleur kept it tied behind her

head in an easy-to-deal-with ponytail, and simply chopped the ends off when it got too long.

She hesitated, and the woman said gently, 'In a sense, Luke is Pacific royalty. He's no snob—he's so completely confident in himself that he doesn't give a damn for image—but you'll be judged against pretty high standards. And—forgive me if I'm speaking out of turn here—you're not like his usual…friends.' She hesitated a second before the final word, leaving it hanging in the air.

Fleur said as easily as she could, 'You're right, of course. Yes, if she can come this afternoon that would be great.'

The woman looked as though she wanted to say more, but a knock at the door heralded Susi, who said that Luke wanted to see Fleur.

In his high-tech office, Luke said calmly, 'We need to talk.'

Heart jumping, she said, 'OK, but I've made an appointment to have my hair cut here in a couple of hours.'

'Good,' he said, his gaze lingering on the bright fall in a sensual assessment that tightened Fleur's skin. 'Make sure she doesn't take too much off. Do you ride?'

The abrupt change from frank male appreciation to a tone of courteous enquiry made Fleur blink. 'Yes, although it's been years since I've been on a horse.'

'It's like swimming; you never forget. Do you feel up to it yet?'

'I'd love to,' she said, her spirits lifting.

He smiled. 'Change into trousers and I'll collect you in ten minutes. Make sure you wear a hat that won't fall off.'

Half an hour later Fleur drew in a deep breath and gazed around. They were riding through a papaya plantation, the big oval fruit hanging in green clusters against the trunks. It was hot, but the horses were acclimatised; Fleur had noticed only a faint sheen of sweat on her mount's chestnut withers, and the mare had plenty more action in her.

'Tell me about yourself,' Luke said. 'Where did you grow up?'

'Waiora, a little town on a tiny harbour on Northland's west coast.'

He nodded. 'What career did you take up?'

'I spent a year at university in Auckland.'

He was wearing an old pair of riding trousers that clung to his heavily muscled thighs like a second skin, and a blue shirt, rolled up to reveal strong forearms tanned the colour of teak. Fleur's heart had performed a couple of erratic orbits when she'd seen him swing up onto a big black gelding after he'd tossed her into the saddle, his hands strong about her waist.

Neither heart nor body had recovered from those

seconds of close contact. She still felt oddly giddy, and it was no use telling herself that it was due to dehydration. It had been years since she'd felt so good, so vital and filled with inner exultation.

He looked down at her, checking on her confidence and her riding ability, she suspected. Fortunately the mare was a darling.

'What degree?' he asked.

'Arts. I wanted to do a history degree.' She amended that to, 'I'll finish it one day.'

His brows lifted. 'I see. Did your mother's illness interrupt your studies?'

She swallowed. 'Yes. When she couldn't look after herself I went back home to care for her.'

'Tough. Was there anyone to help you?'

'No. My parents were divorced when I was ten.'

'Are you in contact with your father?'

'No,' she said briefly, then wondered if she should have perhaps prevaricated a bit on this point. After all, she didn't really know anything about Luke, except what she'd read in newspapers and magazines. For all she knew he could be a white slaver.

She flicked a glance sideways, noting the uncompromising line of his profile, angular and severe. He didn't look like a white slaver. He looked like a man with the world at his feet, a man totally confident in himself—a man born to authority.

A man who knew a lot about women and who

took his impact on them for granted. She'd seen his name linked with more than half a dozen, all glamorous, all moving in the sort of circles that got even the paparazzi excited. And then there was Gabrielle, a model and already in love with him.

So in spite of telling her that he was attracted to her, he certainly wouldn't find Fleur Lyttelton from Waiora, New Zealand, in the least fascinating.

Even if he did, she'd want him to be interested in more than just her body. Though that would be terrifying enough, because her knowledge of men was practically nonexistent. Her year at university had been spent studying and worrying about her mother's increasing ill-health, not living it up socially.

She was still a virgin, for heaven's sake—for all she knew the only twenty-three-year-old virgin in the Pacific Basin!

Anyway, it was too late now for second thoughts, she thought uncomfortably. She'd agreed to this charade and she had to go through with it.

Hurriedly she said, 'My father forced me to choose between him and my mother. He lives in Australia now.'

'Some men don't deserve families.'

'Some women, too.' The male half of the world weren't the only offenders when it came to marital and parental matters. After all, although she was inexperienced she read newspapers and watched television.

She said, 'Tell me what I need to know about you.'

Shrugging, Luke guided his mount up a small slope to stop under a huge old tree, dark-foliaged and heavy of boughs. Behind them the vivid green mountains clawed at the sky, and when she turned her horse to face the view, she caught her breath.

Spread out before them lay a panorama of pure, sun-drenched colour—the bold, bright green of plantations, the softer, more silvery shades of the palm forests by the shore, and the brilliant turquoise of the lagoon bordered by the slashing white line of the reef. And beyond that the blazing, intense emerald of the Pacific as far as she could see, curved around the island like a protective embrace.

Yet there was danger in its limitless expanse.

'I was born here twenty-nine years ago,' Luke told her, not looking at her. 'I expect to die here.'

That simple sentence, said evenly and without emotion, summed up Luke Chapman, revealing perhaps more of him than perhaps he'd be comfortable with. Although he was a man of the world, his roots lay in this exquisitely beautiful place with its lush fertility and its dangers, the untamed sea and sky where cyclones could beat in from a sky of blazing sapphire, leaving behind destruction and death.

His love for Fala'isi was there in his tone, in his crystalline gaze as he looked down on it from their vantage halfway between the mountains and the sea.

He said, 'I ran wild here until my parents sent me to school in New Zealand and to university in England and America. My degree was a business one, but I was more interested in the scope of the Internet than going into conventional business, so I've made my career in that.'

Fleur nodded. The company he'd started in his early twenties to provide an Internet service had grown exponentially. Unlike most entrepreneurs he'd kept control of it, and was now one of the most powerful players in information technology.

He went on, 'However, this is my real life's work—Fala'isi and its people. My father isn't ready to give up his position as head of the family corporation, and I'm not eager to take it on yet, but that's what I'll end up doing.'

Rather daringly she asked, 'Do you want to do that?'

'Wanting doesn't come into it.' Keeping his gaze fixed on the panorama in front of them, he explained in a level, judicious voice, 'I could probably flag it away if my father wasn't also paramount chief. That's a hereditary position—not in that the oldest son or daughter inherits, but the chieftainship is the prerogative of one family. In Fala'isi that's my family. We're the last link with the ancient chiefs of the island, and although our position is more ceremonial than anything else, it's still important. If either of my sisters were interested I might be able to evade the responsibility, but they're not.'

'I'm surprised women would be considered for the position,' Fleur said without thinking.

'Why? Women held—still hold—very high prestige in Polynesian societies. In New Zealand the late Maori Queen was chosen for the position by her people.'

Feeling foolish, she responded, 'I know, and you're right of course. It's just that we—well, I suppose I thought society here would be more rigid than at home.'

'We've always been fairly cosmopolitan,' he said, then changed the subject by pointing out his house, sprawling in its several acres of gardens on a low hill above the lagoon. He added casually, 'Fala'isi is the link between the great prehistoric sailing routes from east to west and north to south. For centuries my ancestors traded and fought and explored along those routes. We islanders pride ourselves on being open to new ideas.'

Although his voice was perfectly level, for some reason the words sounded like a veiled warning. Fleur looked up sharply, met eyes as translucent as polar seas, and felt that odd clutch of response in her stomach, so close to fear it could have been mistaken for it if it hadn't been accompanied by an erotic charge of physical awareness.

All her senses sharpened by Luke's presence, her skin tightening under the impact of his scrutiny, she felt the breath of the breeze as acutely as though she'd been standing in a gale.

'We'd better be getting back,' he said curtly, as though he regretted letting her see even that small bit of his inner thoughts.

Nodding, Fleur turned her mount and pretended to admire the scenery as they rode down towards the house. So this, she thought dazedly, was what sexual attraction was all about. She didn't even know him, yet she'd trusted him when he'd suggested this charade. Had that been because she felt sorry for the girl Luke didn't want, or was it because she was clutching at any straw to stay here in paradise with a man she wanted?

That thought made her feel sick. Was she being a total idiot? Through her lashes she saw him ahead, riding his big gelding with the ease and grace of a man who had spent a lot of time on horseback.

Did he make love with the same cool mastery? Colour burned through her skin, and she had to force herself to concentrate. She was utterly sure her mother hadn't had this dangerous attraction in mind when she'd organised a holiday on Fala'isi for her daughter.

He halted his horse and waited for her to catch up. 'We can ride back along the beach if you like,' he said, then frowned. 'Although you look as though you've caught a bit of sun. Do you want some sunscreen?'

'No, thanks, I'm slathered in the stuff, and I'd love to ride along the beach.'

'No mad galloping,' he said with a hint of irony.

'I've never been into mad,' she told him with perfect truth. 'I was always the one who waited to make sure it was safe before I did anything.'

Even as she said the words she knew their truth— and realised how far she'd strayed from that sensible, if too cautious, attitude.

Luke reached into his shirt pocket and tossed her a tube. 'Sunscreen first.'

Resigned, because he clearly wasn't planning to go anywhere until she'd put more on, she caught it neatly and unscrewed the top. It was warm, mostly from the sun, she told herself sturdily as she smoothed it into her skin. Certainly not from his body...

The thought sent another erotic little shiver through her. Keeping her eyes studiously on the tube, she recapped it and held it out to him. His fingers closed around hers; her mount moved at an involuntary signal from its rider.

'Steady,' she crooned to her horse, and the mare settled.

Luke didn't release her. 'Listen,' he said beneath his breath.

Like a carillon of exquisite purity, a bird sang from somewhere close by.

Enchanted, she listened until the song wound down in a cascade of notes, keeping her eyes on the sight of her hand enclosed in Luke's big, lean tanned one. Time stood still; her breath locked in her throat. She thought dazedly that the sun stopped and no sound of the waves on the reef came to her ears. Even the wild thunder of her heart eased in the haunting, melancholy sweetness of the song. Luke's touch seared through her like the sweetest of daggers, setting off fires in a million unsuspected pleasure points.

Then the notes died away, and she dragged in a breath and pulled, and immediately he let her go.

'That was—superb,' she half said, half whispered. 'It sounded a bit like a kokako—or a tui when it stops mimicking.'

Luke set his horse in motion. 'A *tikau,* native to the island, although I believe it's a distant relative of the kokako. It's a bird of the high mountains and the forest—it rarely comes this close to the sea.' He nodded at a gully to one side. 'It must have lost its way and found some shelter there. I'll have traps set tonight.'

She gazed at him in horror. 'Why?' she demanded.

He gave her a narrow, somewhat cynical smile. 'Because there are predators here—rats, dogs. The bird needs to be taken back to the mountains. It will die here.'

'Oh, I see.'

He indicated a track leading downwards. 'The sea is that way,' he said.

Fleur followed, conscious that something had changed. Gone was the camaraderie of a few minutes ago, replaced by a barrier that hurt her in some obscure way.

The ride along the beach should have been wonderful but although they didn't gallop they cantered, and she suspected that was so he didn't have to talk to her.

Back at the house he said courteously, 'I suggest you have a rest after lunch. Our guests will start arriving at seven.'

'I'll be ready,' she said brightly.

The hairdresser arrived with an assistant. 'Our cosmetics specialist,' she said, and made horrified clucking noises as she examined Fleur's chopped tresses. 'My friend suggested you might like to see a sample of our range.'

'I can't afford any cosmetics,' Fleur said firmly.

The two women looked a little startled, but the hairdresser said, 'We'll give you a free consultation—that is our policy. What you decide to do afterwards is entirely up to you.'

Fleur protested, but both women assured her that whether or not she bought anything was irrelevant.

'So that is settled,' the hairdresser said when Fleur gave in. 'Now, about your hair…'

They discussed the final cut, both women vetoing Fleur's sudden, defiant request for short hair.

'Apart from it being a crime against whatever gene gave you that fabulous hair, it wouldn't suit you,' the hairdresser stated. 'Your eyes and mouth and skin would vie for attention and that wouldn't work at all well. What I suggest is we use that gentle curl and pull the hair back softly to suit your features. Here, I'll show you.'

And Fleur had to agree that she was right.

Just as she had to marvel when she examined her reflection after being made up with cosmetics that smelt subtly of some exotic tropical flower. Somehow, without being obvious, her eyes seemed bigger and much greener, and the lashes she'd thought too pale were now darker and more defined without being spidery. She'd have loved to buy the products, but their quality warned her they'd be expensive.

'They're made on the island, using traditional recipes and scents,' the assistant told her with pride. 'My cousin is the manager. At first we sold only to tourists, but the business is expanding and now we sell to North America and Australia. Mr Chapman— Mr Luke—thinks that Asia will be our biggest market soon.'

'You've done a wonderful job.' Fleur smiled at them, and hoped fervently that they didn't expect a tip. Fortunately, it seemed Fala'isi was like New

Zealand, where tipping wasn't done. 'Thanks so much for everything.'

After the two women left Fleur stared at herself a moment more, before turning away from the mirror in embarrassment. It was foolish to be so charmed by what a skilful cosmetician and some truly wonderful products could do; she couldn't afford them and that was that.

When she went to change her clothes, she stopped, astounded at the sight of rack upon rack of outfits. Everything she'd tried on that morning—not just the ones she'd chosen, but every outfit that had suited her—was there.

Frowning, she spread out the skirt of a silk chiffon evening dress in the softest apricot; it had looked divine, but she'd discarded it because she didn't need more than one outfit for after dark.

She let the silk sift through her fingers, her frown deepening, then turned to the big chest of drawers. Biting her lip, she scrutinised the drawer full of subtly shimmering underwear. The owner of the boutique must have misunderstood.

Well, it would have to go. But halfway down the hall to find Luke she met Susi, carrying a bag of sophisticated blue and green that contained the cosmetics Fleur had just rejected.

'Oh, no!' Fleur stopped. 'There's been some mistake—I didn't buy those.'

'Mr Chapman says they are for you,' the house-keeper said, her smile vanishing.

'No,' Fleur said, flustered yet determined. 'I haven't bought them.'

'But—'

'It's all right, Susi.'

The sound of Luke Chapman's cool, authoritative voice silenced both women. Fleur's heart performed the now-familiar flip, then settled into a more rapid pace.

He held out his hand and the housekeeper gladly relinquished the bag. 'Thanks,' he said, and waited until she'd gone before saying with courtesy, 'Come into my office.'

Fuming, Fleur went with him. Once inside she demanded, 'Did *you* buy these?'

'Yes.' He held up a long-fingered hand and flicked a lock of hair back from her angry face. 'Stop going off the deep end. You're reinforcing a stereotype.'

'That's ridiculous!' she retorted, incensed by her sharp, excited reaction to his nearness. 'You don't know anything about me, and anyway, I've never believed that hair colour had anything to do with temperament. My mother was a redhead and she had the most equable temperament of anyone I've ever known.'

'Did she? I thought red hair was genetically linked to a hair-trigger temper.'

His amused tone told her she'd been distracted by an expert. She drew in a calming breath. 'I didn't buy these cosmetics, and I—'

'Why?'

Distracted again, Fleur blinked. 'What?'

'Why didn't you buy them?' he asked patiently.

'Because I don't need them,' she said, wincing at the note of defiance in her voice. She dragged in another breath and forced her voice into a tone that almost sounded reasonable. 'And I don't need the extra clothes that have miraculously found their way into my wardrobe.'

He shrugged. 'I can afford them. And as you're here because I asked you to stay, and you're entering this charade for my sake, it's up to me to bear the cost.'

'It's the principle of the thing,' she said between her teeth, because she was going to lose this fight, she knew it, and behind the compelling mask of his face he was laughing at her silly little principles. In his world the amount of money the cosmetics and clothes represented was chicken feed, and he was making sure she understood that.

She felt that gulf between them—huge, un-crossable—and it hurt. Which scared her.

'Besides, you need clothes,' he said smoothly, as though paying for her clothes and cosmetics was a perfectly logical thing to do.

Perhaps in his world it was, but for services rendered, she thought waspishly. A shiver of anticipation ran through her at the thought of what those services might be.

Holding her riotous emotions in check, she said more calmly, 'I don't want the clothes and the cosmetics. I know you're trying to be helpful, but I feel—' She stopped again, searching for the right word.

'Bought?' Luke supplied helpfully.

CHAPTER FIVE

FLEUR flinched, her gaze flying to meet his. He didn't look amused now; those angular features were set in a forbidding expression.

'I suppose so,' she muttered, because how idiotic was she being?

'And you're afraid I might demand to be recompensed?' Luke asked in a level voice that didn't hide a disturbing note beneath the cool disdain.

Flushing, she shook her head. 'No!' And, trying to grab some dignity from the situation, she gabbled, 'I don't like being dependent on you.'

'Dependent?' The word rang with irony. 'I suspect that's only part of it. Do you honestly think that I'd go to such an elaborate charade just to get you to stay in my house and—presumably—in my power?'

Put like that, her inchoate suspicions sounded ludicrous. He was experienced; he must know she found him sexually attractive. Hell, she blushed every time he came near her! But he didn't need to be so unforgivably crude as to haul her feelings out into the light of day so he could make her feel stupid and embarrassed.

Proudly lifting her head, she said, 'No, I don't.'

He leaned back and inspected her, his smile arrogant. 'Then what exactly is your problem?'

That infuriating heat scorching along her cheekbones, she set her jaw. 'I'm not a charity case or a Cinderella. I don't need all those clothes.'

'Then don't use them,' he said, allowing a note of impatience in his voice.

'That's not the point. I know I agreed to this, but I'm thinking it's not a good idea.'

'You gave me your word,' he said in a steely voice.

Fleur sent him a quick, startled glance, her spine tightening when she met narrowed eyes and saw his lips compress into a thin, hard line. He looked—dangerous and exceedingly intimidating.

She stiffened. 'And now I'm reconsidering,' she said indignantly. 'I agreed to a—a charade, not a complete loss of autonomy!'

Luke's shoulders lifted in that quick, essentially Gallic shrug. 'I can't, of course, force you to do it.'

His tone was cynical. The heat faded from her skin, leaving her somewhat shaky. He looked as though he'd expected her to do this—agree, then go back on it. And once again, she realised, she'd been steered away from the fact that he'd paid for the clothes and cosmetics she'd discarded. The fact that this time she'd done the steering didn't appease her.

She said, 'I won't wear those clothes.'

'Cutting off your nose to spite your face again?' he said lightly, his smile not reaching those hard eyes. He'd clearly lost interest, and his final remark was tinged with irritation. 'I don't care what you do with them—they're there if you need them. As are the cosmetics. If you want to appear *au naturel,* by all means do so.' He let his gaze roam her indignant face and taut body, and drawled, 'Well, perhaps not entirely. My male guests would probably be delighted if you decided to go completely buff, but I'd rather you didn't.'

He held her gaze for several seconds more, and added with another faint, satirical smile, 'Unless you want to do so for my sole delectation. But, whatever you do, keep the clothes and the cosmetics.'

She said fiercely, 'I don't want them—that's what this is all about! I don't need payment! And although I agreed to this charade, I can't help wondering if it's too close to lying. And lying, even in a good cause, is lying.'

His brows drew together. 'If you really want to back out, that's fine. I don't want you compromising your principles.'

Balked, she stared at him. The silence thickened, gathered into a presence, and finally she made a gesture of surrender. 'You'd make it easier for me if you threatened me,' she finally muttered.

'So you'd give in to threats?' he drawled.

'No, then I could summon up my righteous indignation and storm away and feel good about it. As it is, now I keep thinking about that girl who believes she's going to be your wife. You're probably right, the best way to deal with it and leave her pride intact is to just pretend we're…'

'Lovers,' he said laconically when she came to an abrupt stop. 'Or if that's too much, would-be lovers. Or, even soon-will-be lovers. I don't care.' He held her gaze for several intense moments. 'Let's just take it as it goes, all right? Don't imply anything, don't lie, don't do anything but blush enchantingly whenever I speak to you, and everyone will draw their own deductions without either of us saying a word.'

At the mention of her stupid blushes her cheeks reddened again, and she clapped her hands to them and said in deep mortification, 'One of these days I'm going to learn to control this or die trying.'

'Why? You blush beautifully. Anyway, I believe the tendency fades with more sophistication.'

All pretence at dignity gone, she glowered at him. 'Thank you. You don't have any women's magazines around with pictures, do you, so I can see what Luke Chapman's girlfriend would wear to an intimate dinner party for twenty?'

His smile widened into laughter. 'No, you witch,' he said. 'Just wear what you like—something floaty and light and shortish will do. Tonight's dinner is for a small trade delegation from Australia who are here to try and talk us into letting them prospect for minerals in the mountains, so prepare to be bored. All right?'

'Yes, all right.'

But it wasn't. He'd got his own way with almost indecent ease, and somehow managed to make her even more aware of him—and her own reactions to him—than before.

Luke Chapman was magnetic, and she was perilously close to thinking herself in love with him. Telling herself you couldn't fall in love so quickly didn't help; her brain knew that, but her body persisted in thrilling whenever she thought of him, and her heart was melting ominously fast.

However, she took his advice, choosing the silk chiffon in apricot, but ignored the cosmetics—until a glance in the mirror forced her to realise how naked her face looked with nothing but lipstick. At least cosmetics might camouflage her stupid blushes!

So she unearthed the make-up and did her best to follow the instructions she'd been given that afternoon. It took her a while, but in the end she inspected her reflection with something like relief. She looked all right.

'Well, perhaps a bit better than all right,' she told her reflection, sternly squelching an ignoble satisfaction.

After all, if the guests were connected to the mineral industry surely there wouldn't be anyone to make her feel inferior? They'd be middle-aged men with weather-beaten faces.

Wrong. The first person to arrive was young and tall and gorgeous, with a mane of artfully cut and shaded blonde hair, and clearly she knew Luke very well, embracing him with delight.

Which didn't bore him in the least. He might have avoided the full-blown kiss she was intent on pressing on his lips, but he did it without being obvious, and he kissed both cheeks and then held her at arm's length and said something to her that made her laugh and blush and pat his cheek.

Only then did he introduce Fleur. The gorgeous blonde looked a little puzzled and said, 'I thought you were married—oh, sorry, wrong woman!'

Presumably she meant the mysterious Janna.

At that moment Fleur was devoutly thankful to the woman who'd chosen the clothes for her and to Luke for making her accept the cosmetics. They were armour.

Armour she desperately needed, although Luke gave her unobtrusive but steady support as she negotiated the evening. She even enjoyed the dinner, although when it was over she couldn't remember what she'd eaten.

That might have been because the man beside her, a mining magnate and the most important man in the delegation, turned out to be unexpectedly charming—a man with the soul of a poet when he spoke of the wild, hot, dusty Outback that had made his fortune.

When they'd all gone she said formally to Luke, 'Thank you. You certainly know how to give a dinner party.'

'You seemed to enjoy yourself. Perhaps I should tell you that your dinner partner is very happily married.'

He didn't say it unpleasantly, but she felt a shock of outrage. 'It's not necessary,' she returned with a bite. 'He's old enough to be my father.'

As a riposte it was a cliché, but it was all she could think of.

Luke lifted a black brow to devastating effect. 'Is that important?'

Goaded, she snapped, 'Possibly not to your blonde friend, but it is to me.'

'I was jealous,' he said with cool menace. 'Were you?'

'Jealous?' She stared at him, then coloured and let her lashes fall. 'Neither of us have any right to—to feel anything. Particularly not that,' she said, turning to go.

He touched her bare shoulder and she froze. *No,*

she thought confusedly, looking straight ahead. Tonight he wore a magnificent tropical dinner jacket that emphasised his masculine waist and the lean hips beneath it. It should have looked theatrical; Luke carried it off to perfection.

She tried frantically to haul her thoughts into some sort of order, but her eyes had fixated on the tanned column of his throat, and the arrogant jut of jaw, shaded slightly now by a faint show of beard— and his mouth…

Ah, God, how had she managed to keep her gaze from his mouth for so long?

His lips hardened, then tilted in a smile. 'So why did we both feel it?' he asked, his deep, slightly taunting voice reaching inside her and opening floodgates to release sensations that shook her down to her soul.

Fleur gulped. His hand tightened on her shoulder for a second, then relaxed.

'You smell like the sea,' he said quietly. 'With a hint of frangipani. And when you smile, did you know you have a dimple in your left cheek? It's infuriatingly elusive—it comes and vanishes so quickly it's difficult to catch, but it lends something mischievous to your smile. Were you a mischievous child, Fleur?'

'I don't know,' she croaked. Was there the faintest hint of an accent in the way he said her name? Dimly Fleur remembered his French great-grandmother.

She was having such difficulty concentrating, and all he was doing was talking to her, and resting his hand on her shoulder—well, no, he was sort of caressing it, stroking it as though it was infinitely delightful to his touch...

Tension knotted inside her, holding her in a grip of sensuous enchantment. If something didn't end this delicious stand-off soon, the flames licking through her would consume her and she'd go up like a bonfire. Or do something drastic.

He lifted his hand, and she thought she might be able to breathe again if she stepped back, but she couldn't move.

A lean forefinger came to rest on her cheek, just a bit above her mouth. 'Here,' he said gravely, except that a raw note ran beneath the word, wildly exciting her.

'What?'

'I think the dimple is just here.' And he kissed the spot his finger had touched, his hand sliding across her shoulder in a gesture that shouldn't have been at all carnal.

Her heart went into overdrive, beating high and rapid in her throat and ears, so that all she could hear was his voice as he went on thoughtfully, 'Or perhaps it was here.'

And he kissed her again, this time a little closer to her mouth.

Desire, like a keen longing mixed with incandescent plea-sure, rocketed through her. She stiffened, unconsciously raising her chin so that the kiss grazed the edge of her lips.

On a rough note Luke breathed her name as though it were some kind of talisman, and kissed her aching, eager mouth properly. His lips were firm and warm and compelling as they explored hers. Every thought driven from her head by a charge of pure, unadulterated excitement, Fleur groaned and went limp, and his arms came around her and pulled her into his lean, aroused body.

Stunned, she heard the odd noise she made when he lifted his mouth—part satisfaction, part plea— and she knew he understood it, too. He settled her back against him and kissed her again, and this time she opened her mouth for him, while skyrockets coloured her closed eyelids with the glittering desperation of hunger.

A reckless craving that was reciprocated in spades. She recognised it in the surge of power in his body, the deepening intensity of the kiss, and the burgeoning of his body.

She almost cried out with frustration when he lifted his head again. He took in a huge breath and said in a harsh, intense voice she didn't associate with Luke Chapman, sophisticated man of the world, 'That may well be the biggest mistake I've made.'

'Yes,' she agreed, feeling slightly sick but understanding perfectly.

'Do you regret it?'

Was it her imagination, or did his arms tighten around her? 'No,' she said frankly, adding with even more honesty, 'Although I probably will in the morning.'

'You and me both.' But he laughed quietly as he let her go.

Cold and desolate, Fleur hugged herself until she realised how she must look—pleading, hugely needy—and let her arms drop to her sides. The wildfire heat of a few seconds ago was fading fast, replaced by the chill of his rejection.

'I didn't intend this to happen,' he said abruptly.

'Neither did I,' she said. 'Is that normal?'

He closed his eyes for a second. 'No,' he said, when he opened them again. 'Which is not to say it's abnormal, either. Basically—and this is very basic—I think it's a matter of genes.'

'Genes?' Oh, she knew that. And she knew why he was reminding her—so that she didn't get any stupid ideas about falling in love with him!

His smile was tinged with satire. 'I'm sure you've read science's pronunciation on physical attraction. It's nothing more than our two bodies realising that we'd make superb babies together.'

Colour rolled up into Fleur's skin again. The

thought of having Luke's baby melted some hitherto inviolable part of her. Ignoring it, she said bleakly, 'I know. Just nature making sure the species keeps going. Nothing important at all.'

His eyes narrowed. Flushing, she looked away— away from the colour that rode his striking cheek-bones like a slash of war paint, away from the slightly swollen line of the lips that had taught her in a few short moments what ecstasy could be like, away from the crystalline eyes scanning her face as though she were some new specimen.

From outside came the sound of the *tikau*'s song, each clear cascade of notes echoing in the room.

Luke said something in the local language beneath his breath, and when she stared at him he said in his usual controlled voice, 'I'm sorry. I shouldn't have—I had no intention of touching you. I won't do it again unless it's in public.'

'In public?'

'To keep up the charade we'll have to exchange an occasional significant glance. Possibly even a light—but restrained—caress now and then,' he said, and when she stared at him in dismay, he gave a humourless smile and went on, 'Don't worry, I can control my baser urges when others are around. I've never considered overt displays of lust to be a spectator sport.'

His contemptuous dismissal of the passion she'd

felt hurt ferociously, but she managed to produce a nod.

He said, 'Are you all right for the picnic tomorrow?'

'Yes.' Or as right as she ever would be.

They were taking the mining people to an island that was the Chapman private holiday home. It was to be an informal occasion, with nothing more in mind than the establishing of contacts, some fishing for those who wanted to, and a swim in the lagoon, followed by lunch.

For Fleur it would be a sail into the unknown.

'Hey, this is fabulous!' The blonde woman who'd embraced Luke so heartily the night before stretched languorously on the white lounger and smiled up into a sky that was the bright, brazen blue of a sapphire. Turning her head to look directly at Fleur, she let an envious smile touch her lips and purred, 'Lucky you.'

Fleur said, 'It's glorious, isn't it?'

'So is its owner,' the woman, whose name was Prudence, said coolly. 'You know, I wouldn't have thought you were Luke's type.'

'The world's full of surprises.' Fleur managed a casual shrug and a light, coolly dismissive tone. Her companion's forthrightness startled her, but she knew instinctively that showing astonishment would be seen as a sign of weakness.

'Where did you meet him?'

'At a party,' Fleur said vaguely.

Prudence sat up and began applying sunscreen in slow, voluptuous strokes. 'I don't blame you for being circumspect,' she said, a note of malice tingeing her voice. 'He hates publicity. And maybe you are his type—he does like redheads. Is your hair natural?'

The taunt hit home. 'Every last little wave,' Fleur said, before she had time to think. 'Why? Did you think it was a wig?'

'The colour,' Prudence said shortly. 'You remind me very much of one of his previous lovers— Jenny…no, Janna someone. She was pretty, a model who dabbled in acting. Lots of charm but not a brain in her pretty head. He soon got tired of her.'

The implication couldn't have been more plain. Fleur closed her eyes, opening them a second later when the woman spoke again, this time in a totally different voice. 'Hello, Luke. What a fabulous place.'

Fabulous, Fleur thought snidely, went out in the seventies, surely? Didn't she know any other word? She watched Luke smile, and realised that Prudence had managed to irritate him. Now, how did she know that?

Just something about the quirk of his lips when he said, 'I'm glad you like it.' He looked across at Fleur, and his expression altered subtly. 'How long is it since you put on sunscreen?'

'About half an hour,' she said. 'It's supposed to last two hours.'

'The tropical sun is tough on skin as delicate as yours.' He came over to sit beside her on the lounger. 'Turn your back, and I'll make sure it's covered properly.'

'Would you like me to go?' the other woman enquired archly.

Luke raised his brows. 'Why?' he asked in a pleasant tone, holding his hand out to Fleur for the bottle of sunscreen.

Fleur gave it to him, relieved that he was on her side. He would, she thought, make a bad enemy. He could do more with a slight lift of his brows and a barely perceptible intonation in his deep voice than other men produced with open threats.

Prudence shrugged. 'Oh, I just thought you might need some privacy.'

Luke let the silence last a heartbeat too long before saying, 'No.'

And that was the end of that. Without trying to answer, the other woman waved languidly at someone down the beach before donning her sunglasses and lying back on her lounger. Suddenly cold, in spite of the heat of the sun, Fleur shivered while Luke applied sunscreen to Fleur's back, his hands sweeping the lukewarm liquid across her skin.

She could feel his cold anger, and wondered

why Prudence had provoked it. To make an impression? Possibly. If so, it had backfired—unless Luke would rather be doing this to the other woman and was angry that he had to keep up the pretence with Fleur?

Who cares? she thought bluntly. He'd set this situation up. If he wanted to bed the luscious executive, with her outdated slang and overt willingness, he had only himself to blame that he couldn't.

Although he was anointing her with skill and experience, there was nothing sensual about the slow strokes of his hand. Not for him, anyway. He was doing a job and getting it done as quickly as he could, while through her little rivulets of fire ran from nerve to nerve, sweeping everything before them in honeyed enchantment. Her breath quickened, and she fixed her unseeing eyes on the swimmers in the lagoon.

Until a movement caught her eyes and she said sharply, 'Luke!'

His hand stopped immediately as he followed her line of sight. 'What—?' He bit back an imprecation and got to his feet in one lithe movement.

She catapulted off the lounger, and ran behind him down the white sand and into the water. Although he forged ahead, she swam on, keeping him in sight until he reached deeper water, where he dived.

Thank God the lagoon was as clear as crystal; by

the time she got there he'd already hauled the swimmer—a woman—to the surface, ruthlessly controlling her struggles and holding her head well clear while she coughed and retched.

'I can do this,' Fleur said, panting. 'We need a boat out here.'

Luke demanded, 'Can you keep her upright?'

'Yes.'

'Show me.'

Fleur slid her arm around the swimmer in the classic lifesaver's hold. The woman had stopped struggling and, although she was blue around the lips, her breathing was already stabilising.

Luke said briefly, 'Good girl.' He turned his head to the shore. 'Where the hell is the boat?'

The sound of the engines warned them of its imminent arrival. It came roaring up, stopping rather suddenly when Luke held up his hand in a command that couldn't be ignored.

'All right?' he asked Fleur.

She nodded. 'The West Coast Beaches junior lifesavers would be proud of me,' she said lightly, because the woman in her arms was choking back tears.

Luke smiled. '*I'm* proud of you,' he said, and swam to the idling dinghy, hauling himself over the side with a whoosh that nearly capsized it.

He brought it carefully up to the two of them in the water, where he and one of the crew from the yacht helped the coughing woman into it. Then Luke bent over and hauled Fleur up, holding her for a spectacular second against his sleek, lean body.

'Are you all right?' he demanded, studying her face with half-closed, searching eyes. 'No aftereffects? No exhaustion?'

Surprised, she said, 'No. No, I feel fine. Just a bit puffed, but I haven't been swimming recently.'

And because her body was reacting very oddly to being held in a close embrace, she said, 'Truly, I'm fine. I've fully recovered from my faint.'

'Collapse. Good, let's get ashore,' he said, releasing her after a swift, hard hug.

Back on the beach, the other guests had gathered in a knot just above the wave line.

'We'll use one of the loungers as a stretcher to carry her up to the house,' Luke said. He nodded at Fleur. 'We'll need you.'

The house was small and sparsely furnished, clearly used only for holidays. The four men who'd carried the still weeping woman up set the lounger down carefully in the shade of the terrace and stood around a bit awkwardly.

Addressing one of them, Fleur asked, 'Can you find and bring up her clothes, please?' She looked at the rest of the men and said firmly, 'Thank you so much. I'll come down and let you know when she's ready to have visitors.'

They left, and the woman said between sobs, 'I don't know why I'm crying!'

'Because you're in shock,' Fleur said robustly. 'I've been there—I know what it's like. What you need is a warm shower—'

'Some brandy first,' Luke said, appearing from the house with a small glass. He gave Fleur a swift, challenging grin that curled her toes, then held out the glass to the woman. 'Here, Ms Baxter, drink it down even if you hate it.'

'I do hate it,' she said, 'but I certainly need something!' She drained it, shuddered, and then lay back on the lounger. 'Stupid,' she said wearily, and shivered again. 'I really thought I was going to drown—I swam out to look at the coral and I got cramps in both legs. I've never had it before.'

'How do you feel now?' Fleur asked.

'Better. I only went under twice—Luke dragged me up from the second time. I might have made it up again, but I don't think so. I didn't think anyone had seen me, and I knew the waves on the reef made it impossible for anyone to hear me.'

'Fleur saw you,' Luke said. 'I've just checked with the hospital on the mainland, and they agree that you should be seen as soon as possible, so a chopper is on its way.' He ignored her instant objection. 'Sorry, but that's island policy after an incident like this. There's a risk of serious complication later unless proper medical care is given.' He smiled at her woebegone face. 'I don't think there's anything wrong with you, but a night in hospital will reassure all of us that you're fine.'

His smile seemed to work its usual magic. 'I feel so stupid,' the patient said weakly, lying back and closing her eyes.

'Cramps can happen to anyone,' Fleur said. She smiled down at the woman. 'Would you like me to come with you?'

'I—no,' the woman said, her voice fading. 'You're needed here.'

Luke said easily, 'I'll manage without her.'

'I'll just get our bags,' Fleur said. 'I refuse to go for my first helicopter flight in a bikini.'

His eyes kindled, but he turned and called to one of the staff, his voice sharper than normal.

When the chopper arrived, he said, 'Thank you for this. I've arranged with my PA to attend to all the paperwork, but Sue Baxter is still shocked, and I think she'd like to have you with her at least until she's seen a doctor.'

'I'll be fine,' she said briskly. 'You can't go, and no one else has offered.' Besides, she knew what it was like to wake up in a strange place and wonder where she was and what had happened.

'She's a senior executive from one of the big Australian companies. Unfortunately she's here on her own,' he told her. 'Her company's been notified.'

To her astonishment he bent and kissed her, his arms tightening around her and his mouth taking hers in a dominant stamp of possession.

Flushed and breathless, Fleur hustled into the chopper, and as it rose saw the reason for his final embrace—a woman was watching the chopper pad. Prudence of the hungry eyes and determined mouth. Fleur wondered bleakly if she'd try more of her wiles on Luke.

CHAPTER SIX

SOME hours later Fleur's attention was attracted by a nurse who appeared in the doorway of the private room waving a mobile phone.

Startled, Fleur raised her brows and pointed to her chest. The nurse nodded vigorously. It had to be Luke. Her mouth suddenly dry, Fleur got up from her seat beside the sleeping woman's bed and went across to the door.

'Mr Luke Chapman,' the nurse mouthed, and sighed as she held out the phone.

Handling it rather as if it were a snake, Fleur said into the mouthpiece, 'Hello?'

'Ah, Fleur.' His voice was impersonal, he could have been talking to his PA, but her heart performed an odd revolution before pumping at a much faster pace. 'How is Ms Baxter?'

'She's sleeping now. The tests didn't show any damage, and there's no sign of complications, but the doctors want her to stay in overnight.' Her voice sounded weird, almost croaky, and her pulse picked up even more speed.

'I suspected they would. The chopper's on stand-by if you want to come back.'

So this was how the very rich lived—every available aid waiting for them. She glanced at her watch. 'You're leaving for home in an hour or so, aren't you?' she asked. 'It doesn't seem worth it.'

'I'll collect you myself, then. Don't leave the hospital until I come.'

He spoke perfectly normally, yet a barely discernible undertone in his voice lifted the hair on her skin. 'Why?'

After a pause so slight she wondered if she'd imagined it, he told her, 'Because the last time you were let out on your own you collapsed. Humour me, all right?'

Fleur swallowed. 'OK,' she said tautly. 'I'll stay put.'

'Thank you,' he said. 'See you soon.'

Fleur switched off the phone and went to the door, noticing for the first time the tall islander standing on the other side of the corridor. He smiled respectfully, and she realised with a jolt that he was security of some sort. She smiled back and set off to the nurses' station with the telephone.

'All right?' the nurse asked, looking up from sheets of paper.

She nodded. 'Mr Chapman wanted to know how Ms Baxter is.'

'She'll be fine,' the nurse said professionally, eyeing Fleur with interest. 'He's a good man, Luke Chapman—sexy, too! You look a bit stiff when you move. Did you drag her out?'

'Helped,' she admitted.

The nurse said, 'You look as though you need a shower. Why don't you use the bathroom down the corridor—it's well past the patients' showering time.'

Accustomed to the protectiveness with which her mother's hospital had guarded its facilities, Fleur said uncertainly, 'Will that be all right?'

'Of course!' The nurse grinned. 'The Chapman family set up this hospital and they provide a lot of money for its running. In fact, there's some big charity do soon that's fundraising for a cancer ward here. Nobody's going to object if you use a bit of our water and electricity.' She eyed Fleur. 'Are you keeping up your water intake?'

'How did—?' Fleur stopped, because of course everyone on the island would know by now that she'd fainted dramatically in front of Luke's car. And if they didn't know that, they certainly knew she'd been living in his house.

The nurse laughed. 'Oh, like any small community we keep tabs on people, but I'll make sure some lime juice goes to Ms Baxter's room for you. Keep drinking it—we don't want Mr Luke mad at us for not looking after you.'

The power of the Chapman name, Fleur thought as she collected her bag on the way to the bathroom. Not just here on their home territory, either. If she'd learned anything during her stay here, it was that Luke was sought after by people all around the world.

The shower was bliss, and the iced lime juice waiting in the ward was delicious, too. Not quite so good was the fact that after checking Sue Baxter out, the doctor insisted on doing the same for Fleur, finally saying, 'What it is to be young and healthy. You're in good shape, but have a rest every afternoon, and—'

'Keep drinking,' Fleur chorused with her. 'Thanks very much for everything you've done for me.'

After that she joined Sue Baxter in her room. When she woke they chatted quietly, and during the long intervals when the patient slept Fleur read a variety of magazines—mostly elderly—while the afternoon slipped by. None of them, she was grateful to discover, had anything about Luke in them, although his beautiful sisters featured largely in one that reported a very aristocratic ball and wedding in England.

Eventually the door into the private room opened to reveal Luke, big and totally competent, accompanied by the hospital superintendent.

The following ten minutes were filled with Sue's attempt to express her appreciation to both Luke and Fleur.

She ended by saying, 'You've done enough now—off you go, Fleur, and have some fun. I'm so sorry for spoiling your day!'

'Please don't say that,' Fleur said, and bent to kiss her cheek. 'I'm glad you're feeling better.'

'Just relax and let us look after you,' Luke said. 'Someone will be here tomorrow morning to help you, and if the doctor agrees you'll be taken back to Australia tomorrow afternoon. All you have to do is get better.'

'My boss will want to thank you,' Sue said, her lashes drifting down. 'And so will I—coherently—when whatever they've given me finally wears off and I can keep my eyes open for more than five minutes!'

Outside, Fleur waited while Luke spoke to the superintendent, then the security guard escorted them down in the lift to the car park beneath the modern building.

And there a journalist lurked. Young, rather earnest, he approached a little diffidently.

Although Luke frowned, he listened to his request for information. To Fleur's surprise he said, 'One of my guests got cramp while swimming and had to be airlifted back to hospital. She's fine now. Miss

Lyttelton rescued her and stayed with her until she was comfortable.'

The reporter looked even more diffidently at Fleur. 'You are a lifeguard, miss?' he asked.

'I trained with a surf lifesavers' club when I was growing up in New Zealand,' she said, wondering how much Luke would be expecting her to say. 'But Mr Chapman is being very modest—he got to her before I did. All I did was help him.'

'If I could have a photograph…?' the reporter suggested, his expression revealing that he expected to be turned down.

But Luke shrugged. 'If you want one.'

So he and Fleur posed for a photograph against the blank wall of the hospital, and the journalist went away happy.

The car had darkened windows, and as they were driven off Fleur said, 'If that's the local paparazzi you breed reporters differently on Fala'isi.'

'Don't be fooled,' Luke returned. 'He's an extremely clever, persistent man, and the fact that he was waiting for us makes me wonder what he's heard.'

She glanced at him. His expression was hard and intent, as though he was mentally running through a variety of options, none of which he found satisfactory.

Intrigued, she asked, 'What he's heard? Do you mean about the possibility of exploring for minerals?'

'Not necessarily,' he said, but absently. Then he seemed to remember who he was talking to. 'I have a hunch,' he explained with uncharacteristic vagueness, and gave her a smile of such blazing charm it made her toes curl and set off a cathedral full of warning bells.

It wasn't fair that he could use his inbuilt magnetism to scramble her brain and send secret, forbidden messages to every part of her body.

Trying to ignore that most intimate betrayal, Fleur sent him a direct look. She had a hunch, too— that he was evading some issue. 'I wouldn't have thought you dealt much in hunches. Logic seems more your line.'

'My father has a saying—when logic fails, follow your instinct.'

'And does logic often fail?'

'Very rarely, but when it does, I take his advice. So far it's worked.' He shrugged again. 'Thank you for everything you did this afternoon.'

'You've already thanked me, and so has Sue. It was nothing,' she returned. 'Somebody had to go with her, and if you had I'd have had no idea how to deal with all those people.'

He inspected her face in a long, slow survey that sent little chills across her skin. His unusually grey eyes were almost translucent, yet she thought they could see right through her.

'You'd have coped,' he said finally. 'You have a definite talent for organisation and quick thinking.'

Pleasure pinked her cheeks. Flippantly she said, 'When I leave I might ask you for a reference saying just that. As for thanks—you should thank the life-saving association—or send them a donation. In New Zealand we don't have paid lifeguards.'

His lashes drooped. 'I'll suggest Sue's company donates to the lifeguards,' he said. 'Why do you need a reference?'

'I have to find a job.'

'Is it likely to be difficult?'

'No.'

It was the truth; her old job in a fast food shop was waiting for her if she wanted it. Or she could do the work her mother's illness had trained her for—work in a rest home or take nursing training.

Whatever, one day she'd finish her degree and find a job that would pay off the student loan she'd have to increase.

'You're not telling me the truth,' he said shrewdly, and took her chin in his hand, turning it so that he could scrutinise her face.

Thoughts danced crazily in her brain. She stared at his mouth, cruelly beautiful, sculpted to seduce and woo, and her heart flipped and her blood sang in her ears.

Unable to speak, her lips formed one word. 'Don't.'

Followed, when he still stared at her as though trying to drag her soul from her body, by another word. 'Please,' she whispered.

Luke let her go, his hand falling to his thigh, where it clenched into a fist. After a moment he said harshly, 'You pack a hell of a punch, Fleur.'

She did? Fleur swallowed to ease her dry throat. 'So do you,' she said with bleak honesty, and scrambled for another subject, anything to relieve the tension that crackled between them.

Staring out of the window, she realised the car had just gone past the gates of his parents' house. Relieved, she blurted, 'You said your parents were away. Are they on holiday?'

'Having another honeymoon,' he said, his tone telling her that he knew exactly what she was doing.

She managed a cracked little laugh. 'Sounds romantic.'

'They're a very romantic couple,' he said coolly. 'A testament to the fact that two strong-willed people can live happily together.'

'Some people have all the luck,' she said on a flippant note.

'Luck?' He considered the word. 'Luck that of all the people in the world they met at the right time, perhaps. But after that it isn't luck that makes a marriage like theirs.'

Did he believe in the romantic ideal? If his

parents were still lovers after many years, possibly he did—and possibly she might, too, if she hadn't seen first-hand how marriages could shatter, leaving nothing but shards of lives. Her father had believed in romance—she remembered huddling in her bed as he'd told her mother, not wanting to hurt her yet unable to resist the great passion he'd found.

'Good for them,' she said brightly as the car drew up outside the porticoed front entrance of his house.

Once inside he said, 'The charity dinner I told you about is being held here tomorrow night. It will be followed by an after-dinner dance at a mystery venue. Wear something elegant with sparkles.'

'Is there anything I can do to help?' she asked tentatively.

'I shouldn't think so.' He scrutinised her. 'How are you feeling now?'

'Fine,' she said a little blankly. 'I seem to have fully recovered from dehydration. I just feel a bit tired, that's all. I think the doctor was overreacting when she said I shouldn't go home yet.'

He shrugged, penetrating grey eyes still scrutinising her face. 'I don't. And tonight I suggest you have dinner in your bedroom and go to bed early. Tomorrow night is likely to be very late, although of course we can come home if you get tired.'

He went on, 'Gabrielle and her grandfather are

arriving mid-morning. They're bringing another couple—friends of mine—with them.'

The second couple of friends turned out to be royalty—Prince and Princess Guy of Dacia, an island realm in the Mediterranean. Thrown this bombshell when Luke introduced them, Fleur wondered feverishly if she should curtsey, but a few moments spent talking to them soothed her. They were charming, the Princess a tall Englishwoman with milk-white skin and black hair and eyes like silver crystals, while her even taller husband's face and tawny eyes revealed his Mediterranean heritage.

'You're from Northland?' the Princess—Lauren— said enthusiastically. 'Oh, it's a gorgeous place. I've spent some wonderful holidays in the Bay of Islands. Do you know Lucia Radcliffe?'

'I've heard of her,' Fleur said noncommittally.

Her home village on the wild west coast of Northland was an hour's drive and another world away from the cosmopolitan tourist centre of the Bay of Islands. She had never met—or even seen—the Dacian princess who'd married a New Zealander and appeared in magazines from time to time, although never of her own choice. Apparently she was very happy with her two children and her handsome tycoon of a husband on their huge estate in the hills north of the Bay.

Lauren smiled. 'She loves New Zealand, too. How are you enjoying Fala'isi?'

This she could deal with. 'Who wouldn't? It's my first visit to the tropics, and it's even more beautiful than the photographs.'

'Isn't it just!' But the Princess's smile slipped a little, and her husband was instantly at her elbow.

Luke said to the couple, 'I'll show you to your room.' He looked at Fleur and gave her a slow, heart-stopping smile that melted her bones. 'Perhaps you could order tea for us all out on the terrace.'

Which left Fleur entertaining an elderly Frenchman whose keen eyes saw too much, and his granddaughter, a beautiful creature who viewed her with a mixture of irritation and aristocratic hauteur.

As Fleur led the way out onto the terrace and seated them, she wondered how on earth she'd let herself be talked into this masquerade. Damn Luke and his calm assumption that the world was his to command!

And stupid her, for letting him override her sensible reservations.

Fortunately both Gabrielle and her grandfather had exquisite manners, and all three were talking easily—if with some reserve—when the others came back without the Princess, who'd decided to rest until lunchtime.

Was she pregnant? Fleur wondered, and was horrified at the pang of longing that consumed her. Fighting it, she concentrated on the guests.

Lunch passed pleasantly, but afterwards in her room she allowed herself a small sigh. The Prince and Princess weren't publicly demonstrative, but their feelings for each other burned like a smouldering fire.

It was foolish and ungracious to let others' happiness make her envious, especially as such relationships were the exception rather than the rule—well, according to gossip columnists, anyway.

So she'd banish this feeling of being the odd one out, and organise herself for the night ahead. At the thought of dancing with Luke reckless heat consumed her, melting her bones and bringing a dangerous, decadent smile to her lips.

Oh, it would be wonderful. And terrifying. So she had to make sure he didn't realise just how wonderful and terrifying.

A knock at the door brought her around. It was the maid, her pleasant face creased and anxious.

'What is it?' Fleur asked.

'I'm sorry, miss, but I can't find Mr Luke, and the tuna hasn't come for the dinner and the cook is angry.'

'Mr Luke's gone riding with the Prince,' Fleur said. 'All right, I'll come along.'

It appeared that the most essential part of the

dinner menu, the specially caught and sliced tuna, hadn't arrived, and no one could tell the apoplectic chef where it was.

'It has to be marinated in lime,' he explained at the top of his voice. 'If it doesn't get here soon it will be too late and then everything will be ruined.'

'Everything won't be ruined because you'll already have made another starter,' Fleur said firmly. 'I'm quite sure that someone with your experience and your skills can do that and still make it a meal to remember.'

He said sulkily, 'But *everything*—the wine, the menu—has been specially chosen to meld together to make one perfect meal. Any alteration—any deviation—will bring the whole wonderful edifice crashing down.'

Fleur let her brows drift upwards. 'Are you telling me you can't produce another starter that's just as suitable?'

'Of course I'm not,' he said explosively, 'but I am telling you that Mr Chapman will have to choose another wine and it will have to be chilled.'

'I'll make sure that he knows the problem the moment he gets back from the stables,' she said soothingly. 'What suggestions do you have for an emergency starter?'

He frowned, and rattled off several alternatives. Surmising that any hesitation on her part would be a bad thing, Fleur chose the only one she recognised. 'The onion tart.'

He shrugged, obviously handing over all responsibility to her. 'So, it is decided,' he said, and turned away to begin barking at the kitchen staff in the island tongue.

Hoping fervently she hadn't made things worse, Fleur made her way out of the kitchen. The place had been a revelation—huge and ultra-modern, with air-conditioning to cool it. Clearly Luke recognised the value of looking after his staff.

She found the housekeeper competently supervising the setting of a table out on the terrace.

After a quick explanation, Susi said, 'Of course I will see that a message is left for Luke in the stables.'

No one came to her with any other emergency, so she concluded that the cook had done whatever needed to be done.

After she'd dressed for dinner she ventured forth, feeling incredibly glamorous in a camisole gown that matched her skin. She'd been a bit worried that the ivory silk clung too closely to her curves, and perhaps the neckline showed more cleavage than she was comfortable with, but after sinking her principles enough to try on several other dresses she settled on it because it would move from dinner table to dance floor with grace.

She was walking past the door to Luke's bedroom

when it opened and he emerged, darkly saturnine in evening clothes.

Her wayward heart picked up speed.

'I hear you dealt with an emergency,' he said, examining her in a way that sent prickles of pleasure through her.

She managed a laugh, horrified when it emerged low and breathy. 'I think your cook just needed to be comforted because the tuna hadn't turned up.'

'Susi told me you handled him like a pro. Put him on his mettle, then chose the one dish he's famous for.'

'Did I?' She laughed more naturally and confessed, 'That was a lucky break. I chose it because it was the only one I recognised.'

'All he wanted was to have his dilemma recognised and to be challenged to work a miracle—you clearly read him perfectly.' Beneath his amused words ran an intoxicating thread of awareness.

'Just as well he didn't need any real help, because I don't know anything about *haute cuisine*. I can do good plain farmhouse fare, and that's it.'

Together they went along to the big reception room that overlooked the lagoon and the western horizon. But once inside he frowned down at her. 'You look exquisite, but you need something else to go with that gown. Come with me.'

'I'm fine.'

'Every other woman here,' he told her, 'will have jewellery. Serious stuff.'

She shook her head. 'I don't own any and I couldn't wear anything of your mother's,' she said carefully, rebelling at the thought of being tricked out in jewellery to appease his pride. For once he wasn't going to get his own way; besides, it didn't ring true. Luke had far too much confidence in himself to worry about what others would think.

'I'm not going to give you anything of my mother's,' he said curtly. 'I don't have the right. But I inherited some from my great-grandmother, and some I've acquired—we grow pearls here, in case you didn't know. And tonight we need to convince everyone that this relationship is serious enough for me to part with some of my pearls.'

When she bit her lip, he said a little impatiently, 'Don't be silly, Fleur. Think of them as a prop in a play.'

'Do you always get your own way?'

'Usually,' he replied with a straight face. 'It comes of being the only boy in the family, I think. My sisters spoiled me.'

Not just his sisters either, she thought wryly as she went with him into a small strongroom off his office. Probably every woman he met had a strong inclination to spoil him in their various ways.

Including her.

And she *was* being silly; as he'd said, the pearls were simply a prop, so why was she so reluctant to borrow them?

Because, she realised with a panicky intake of breath, she wanted anything he gave her to mean something.

This was getting out of hand. She'd always been aware of him as a man, but his searing kiss had woken her sleeping body, fundamentally transforming every cell. Now when she looked at him or thought of him it was with a secret inner yearning, a fierce hunger that ate away at her self-sufficiency.

She had to stop it right now.

CHAPTER SEVEN

TENSELY Fleur watched Luke open a safe and pull out a handful of cases. He flicked up the lids of a couple, and brought them across to her. 'Which do you like best?'

Afraid that he might read the apprehension in her eyes, she kept them fixed on the jewels. Exquisite, lustrous with a faint golden sheen, one was a string of perfectly graduated and matched beads. The other featured a single magnificent tear-shaped pearl, the gold chain fastened by a diamond clasp.

'They're the same colour as your skin,' Luke said. 'The pendant, I think, will sit better in the neckline of your dress.' He closed one box and put it back in the safe.

'Turn around,' he commanded.

When she obeyed, Luke brushed her firefall of hair aside and thought that there was something oddly vulnerable about the nape of a woman's neck. Not that he'd call Fleur defenceless, he thought with a twist to his lips as he dropped the pendant around her throat and fastened the clasp, his hands lingering a fraction of a second too long on her exquisite skin.

Far from defenceless, in fact; she stood up for herself, and had been extremely competent in two different emergencies, yet something about her made him intensely protective.

As well as aggressive and reckless and aroused.

Possibly it was her natural perfume, the faint, barely noticeable aroma that sent a surge of involuntary heat through him whenever he got close to her. Pheromones, he thought cynically, and recalled the time he'd reminded her of the primal signalling system that ensured two people would make healthy babies.

Not that he was thinking of making babies with Fleur Lyttelton! Making love—now, that had been occurring to him with more and more frequency since he'd first met her. However, he knew how to master his urges.

Usually...

Frowning, he set the clasp on her skin, charmed to see a faint blush of colour stealing through it. Luke swept the bright flood of her hair to cover the clasp and in full control of his voice said, 'There.'

And allowed himself to turn her around so that he could see the effect.

Her blush was full-blown by now, and her lack of

experience charmed him, too. An image burst full-blown into his mind—Fleur in his bed, wearing nothing but the pearl, lax and sated in a tangle of sheets, her green eyes heavy-lidded, her spectacular mouth slightly swollen from his kisses, her breasts still rosy from his caresses.

And her hair across his chest, a silken river of fire.

He released her and stepped back, his voice harsh as he said, 'Perfect. There are earrings, too.'

She shook her head, her eyes far cooler than her skin, her mouth compressing. 'That would be overkill,' she said succinctly, and turned and walked out of the strongroom.

For some primitive reason it irritated him that she didn't bother to check herself out in a mirror. Shoulders held straight, she walked beside him into the main reception room, stopping inside the door at the sound of Gabrielle's voice from somewhere behind them.

When Luke noticed the subtle stiffening of his companion's body, that odd protectiveness surged through him again. He rested his hand lightly in the small of her back and said crisply, 'You look exquisite, and you have excellent manners and a talent for coping. As my indomitable French great-grand-mother used to say in similar situations, *en avant!*'

Forward! Supported by his understanding, she turned her head and smiled at him. He was heartbreakingly attractive, his intimate, complicit smile implying that they were in this together, the arrogant framework of his face set off by faultless tailoring and the white shirt beneath his dinner jacket.

For a taut second his unsparing gaze rested on her mouth before he commanded, 'Just smile, Fleur. That's all you need to do.'

'Be a good little decoration, you mean?' she flashed back.

He grinned. 'You're very decorative, but, no, there's something about your smile that makes people instinctively trust you.' Eyes glinting, he finished, 'In fact, that smile would make you the perfect con artist.'

Startled, she stared at him before spluttering into laughter. 'You certainly know how to give with one hand and take away with the other!'

So when Gabrielle and her grandfather arrived it was to find their host and his presumed mistress laughing at each other. Meeting Gabrielle's angry gaze, Fleur wondered if he'd deliberately teased her to create just that sense of spurious intimacy.

Probably.

The evening opened before her like a flower unfolding. She found herself introduced to a mixture of islanders and people from around the world—people whose names she recognised from the financial press, gossip columns and film reviews.

She'd have hated to be dismissed as Luke's latest inamorata, but his power seemed absolute; her supposed position in his life meant that she was treated with respect.

At one stage she talked to a hot new star whose last blockbuster film had just revealed that he could really act as well as ripple his muscles; a native of Fala'isi, he turned out to be a cousin of Luke's. He told her of his desire to play Othello some day. A short time later she was discussing books with the head of a huge investment firm and his wife.

She kept an eye on the guests, making sure no one was ever alone; it wasn't too onerous, as they were a close-knit group who knew each other well. Even Gabrielle seemed to forget her shock at finding another woman in residence; Fleur relaxed when she saw her and the film star engaged in flirtatious banter.

Instinctively Fleur searched out Gabrielle's grandfather; he was watching his granddaughter with a frown. He met Fleur's quick glance and the frown deepened.

Worried, she turned back to the woman she was conversing with. Almost immediately they were joined by Luke. Overt displays of affection clearly weren't his style, but he used the power of his personality to create an aura of sexual chemistry between them with nothing more than a few fleeting, proprietary touches and an understated possessiveness.

And when their eyes met no one within seeing distance could have missed the sizzle. Of course with him it was staged; unfortunately her responses were only too real.

Wildfire sensations clamouring through her treacherous body after another intent, steel-grey glance, Fleur no longer cared about the guests; she just hoped that Luke thought her acting was on a par with his.

After half an hour he said quietly, 'Dinner's ready.'

'With or without tuna, I wonder?'

He picked her hand up and dropped a light kiss on her palm, folding her fingers over it as though to keep the kiss safe. 'Help me get them to the table.'

Rivulets of fire ran through every nerve. The noise of conversation faded; she stared up into eyes that were half closed and gleaming with desire.

And then he put her hand down and said, 'That should convince anyone who wasn't already persuaded. You're doing wonders, Fleur.'

Hoping she successfully hid the bitter chagrin that doused her, she said numbly, 'So are you.'

But the reminder was necessary. All of this was fake, playing to an audience. She respected Luke for his chivalry towards someone who clearly meant a lot to him, but he wasn't the one who'd have to pay the price.

The masquerade seemed likely to cost Fleur her heart.

Dinner was served on the terrace. Susi and her team had risen splendidly to the occasion, decorating the table in a flamboyant, very Pacifika style with great clusters of flowers and fruit. Wineglasses and silver sparkled in the light of candles, and the scent of night-blooming flowers permeated the air with lazy, overt sensuality.

A fountain whispered and glinted in the glow of subdued lights that glowed on great shiny leaves and flowers. And above it all rose the moon, huge and golden in a cloudless sky where unknown stars mingled with familiar ones.

Luke didn't put her in the hostess's position at the other end of the table; that position was reserved for the Princess. Instead Fleur sat at his right hand.

The dinner was already a success. Yet in spite of everything, she had never felt so alone in her life. Then her gaze fell onto the tuna that had miraculously arrived in time to be marinated in lime and chili with tomatoes. Lifting her lashes, she met Luke's eyes, laughing as they exchanged silent messages, and her heart squeezed into a tight ball of pleasure mixed with foreboding.

Emotions sang through her, a seething tumble of excitement and desperate anticipation. Aware that people were covert-ly watching, she looked back down at her plate, and in full knowledge of the probable consequence—heartbreak—made the most reckless decision of her life.

This was something out of a dream; just this once she'd let herself enjoy everything without hedging the experience with fear. After all, broken hearts mended. Even her mother, still loving the man who'd betrayed them, had found happiness of a sort after his departure. She'd never been able to love another man, but they'd had years of contentment together until her illness struck.

'So it arrived in time,' Luke said beneath his breath.

She smiled radiantly at him, welcoming the swift narrowing of his eyes. 'Thank heavens. Does he do this sort of thing regularly?'

'He's difficult. And of course he knows his own worth—people have been trying to tempt him away for years, and he doesn't really like living in the tropics. Every so often he makes plans to open a café in Provence.'

Fleur swallowed her first mouthful. 'He's a genius,' she said on a sigh of pure delight. 'You have to allow geniuses their tantrums.'

'Well, you certainly managed his superbly. But then, as I told you before, I suspect that you have a talent for coping.' He smiled at her.

She'd rather have a talent for being a wonderful hostess, or making scintillating conversation. 'It wasn't really a problem. He just wanted to vent—and for someone else to take responsibility.'

Luke eyed her with something like respect. 'You don't miss much. That's why the little café in Provence will never lure him away from here—he doesn't like responsibility. Whereas you seem to know how to deal with it.'

'It's easy when it's not really my affair,' she returned coolly, reminding him that she was there on a strictly temporary basis.

He nodded. 'Possibly, but you showed no hesitation about helping me with Sue Baxter. She sends her regards and her thanks, by the way, and her company is exceedingly grateful to you. I suspect a gift is on its way.'

Fleur frowned. 'I did no more than anyone else would have done,' she said crisply. 'I don't want anything for simple human compassion.'

'I did suggest the surf lifesaving club,' he said with an ironic lift of one brow, 'and I think they're doing something about that, but Sue wanted a more personal expression of her thanks as well.'

Without waiting for an answer he turned to the woman on his other side, leaving Fleur feeling not only ungrateful but ungracious.

Especially as a small part of her reason for accompanying Sue Baxter to hospital was that she'd felt ill at ease with the company on the beach.

Oddly enough, not so much here. Whether it was the silk dress, or the magnificent pearl that warmed her throat, or even Luke's close company, she didn't know, but she felt more able to deal with the situation.

'How long have you known Luke?' the man beside her enquired cheerfully.

Wishing he'd chosen another topic, she smiled at him. 'Not very long.'

'But long enough?'

He was slightly older than Luke, she guessed, and disposed to be friendly, viewing her with an approving eye. 'Yes,' she admitted, aware that another of her wretched blushes was heating her cheeks. 'Are you from Fala'isi?'

'An islander born and bred. I grew up with him here,' he told her. 'He was one tough kid. He could ride any horse on the island, surf any wave, jump off any cliff into any sea—just keeping up with him exhausted the rest of us. I think his mother wondered what on earth she'd given birth to.'

Fleur kept her gaze firmly away from the man under discussion. 'I can imagine,' she said demurely.

'Ah, well, he learned to control those daredevil impulses—he's a Chapman, and self-discipline is a big thing for them. But they were great times.' He looked appreciatively at her. 'I see you're wearing the Goddess's Tear.'

'What—oh, the pendant?' She glanced down at the exquisite thing.

'That's the one. I remember the day it was found—fifteen years ago. My cousin dived for it and brought it up. It's beyond price—utterly flawless—and there's no other thing like it in the world. The moment we saw it we knew what we'd call it. There's a legend around the name.'

'I suppose legends go with the territory?'

He grinned. 'Absolutely. Luke bought the Tear. I knew he'd had it set as a pendant, but I don't think anyone—not even his mother or his sisters—has ever worn it.'

So that was what Luke had meant when he'd said he wanted to convince everyone that this was a serious relationship. Making sure she wore something so precious would certainly do the trick in this group.

The stone around her neck seemed to grow heavier. Now that she realised its value and rarity she felt branded, as though Luke had somehow stamped her with a sign of possession.

A prop, he'd called it—an extremely expensive and precious prop!

Her companion asked, 'What did he tell you about the local pearls, the golden pearls of Fala'isi?'

'Not a lot.'

'They're completely unique. They grow in the

lagoon of an atoll fifty miles or so from the main island here, and nowhere else.'

'Nowhere in the world?'

'Nowhere. And if you try to transplant them they die. No one knows why. They're also extremely difficult to use for culturing—for some reason the oyster doesn't react like others do, so their pearls are hugely valuable. Yours was found on the first day of the new year—the Polynesian new year, that is.'

'Matariki,' she said, nodding.

He looked surprised. 'Oh—of course, you're a New Zealander. Yes, the day the Pleiades rise in the east. Of course pearls with that superb lustre and soft golden colour play can only be worn by women with a certain skin tone—luckily for you, you have it.'

Intrigued, Fleur asked more questions about the pearl industry.

It transpired that he ran the local end of it, and with her encouragement he waxed eloquent about the advances that had been made in harvesting and safety and marketing.

When she turned to talk to Luke again she met eyes the burnished colour of a sword blade, cold and intimidating with a lick of blue flame in their depths. Her heart contracted into a tight ball in her chest, but she met his formidable gaze with slightly raised brows and a level glance.

His smile was cool and cynical. 'Enjoying yourself?'

'Very much,' she returned with a tight smile. 'I've just been hearing what an adventurous childhood you had. Your parents must have been thankful when you finally grew up still in one piece.'

'My mother was. My father was apparently just as reckless.' He paused, letting his gaze drift down to the pearl around her throat. 'What else have you learned?'

'That this pretty thing is rare and very precious.'

'Very suitable,' he said, his flat, lethal tone contradicting the words.

What the hell had got into him? Temper brought swift colour to her cheeks. She took a deep breath and returned sweetly, 'How kind.'

He laughed and put his hand over her clenched one on the table. Shocked at a gesture so public, she tried to pull away, but his fingers tightened. He didn't hurt; his cool gaze let her know that any release would be his decision.

And then she was free and he said in a different voice, 'Did he happen to mention that I have a nasty temper?'

'No, but I know now,' she said sweetly, refusing to give an inch.

Luke's laughter sounded genuinely unforced. Fleur watched him and something inside her melted and dissolved, and she realised that it was too late to worry about the state of her heart. It was already dangerously compromised.

When Luke sobered she asked quietly, 'What was that all about?'

'I think it must be that emotion we're not allowed to feel,' he said, looking at her with what must have appeared to anyone watching to be amusement mixed with a certain spice of lust and affection.

Jealousy? Fleur's skin tightened, but he turned to his partner and the moment was over.

In the car on the way to the after-dinner function, Lauren Bagaton said, 'Luke, that was a fabulous meal. And such fun! What a terrific way to make money for charity—a dinner with good friends in the most romantic place in the world. Well, apart from Dacia, of course!'

'I'm glad you enjoyed it, and we have Fleur to thank for saving it from disaster,' he said dryly.

Fleur said, 'Nonsense!'

But Lauren demanded to know what had happened, her laughter pealing out when Luke obliged.

Her husband Guy asked, 'Where are we going?'

'It's a deep, dark secret,' Luke said lightly.

'On Fala'isi? Don't expect us to believe that—you know everything that happens here.'

Luke smiled. 'I've been sworn to discretion. You'll just have to wait until we get there. It's not far now.'

And although Lauren coaxed, he refused to say

anything more. 'It's a surprise,' he said, adding, 'If I tell you I'll be hung, drawn and quartered by the committee of women who've worked so hard to make the evening a success.'

'You're afraid of a committee?' Lauren asked, laughing.

'You don't know these women,' Luke told her cheerfully. 'You'll just have to wait until we get there.'

There turned out to be a pavilion overlooking a magnificent beach. Built and decorated just for this occasion, a dance floor shrouded by white silk walls had been looped with garlands of golden-hearted frangipani and hibiscus. Tables under the stars overlooked the lagoon, and a band tuned up for the hundred or so people who'd been brought there from dinner parties all over the island. Light from hundreds of candles warmed the moonlight.

Lauren said to Fleur, 'We can get our make-up touched up in that tent over there. Coming?'

'Yes,' she said, fascinated by this intimate glimpse into social life amongst the very powerful.

In the tent several women from a famous cosmetics firm were working their esoteric magic.

One took Lauren and another whisked Fleur into a chair. 'With skin like that you don't need more cosmetics, but how about a little extra something to bring out the green in your eyes?'

'Not green eyeshadow, please!' Fleur implored.

The woman laughed. 'I swear, no green eye-shadow.'

She worked skilfully for several minutes, and then held up a mirror. 'There.'

Fleur stared at her reflection. Her lips were sinfully exotic in a coral that she'd never have dared to wear because it should have clashed with her hair. And her eyes—oh, her eyes were greener than she'd ever seen them, the clear, mysterious green of the wild ocean, and they seemed bigger and darker and infinitely more inviting.

'How did you do that?' she asked, amazed.

'Come to the salon one day and I'll show you.' The woman brushed aside her thanks and turned to the next eager partygoer.

Lauren was waiting for her, looking brighter than she had before. 'Aren't they clever?'

'She said she could teach me how to do this.' Immediately after Fleur said the words she wished she hadn't—they made her sound naïve and out of place.

But Lauren smiled and took her arm. 'Then let her. Make-up is fun. Now, where are our men?' Taller than Fleur, she looked around. 'Ah, here they come.'

The two men materialised through the throng of people, both turning heads as they came. For the first time in her life Fleur was the recipient of envious looks from other women. A forbidden excitement unfurled from the tight knot of anticipation in her chest. Soon there would be dancing…

She accepted a glass of champagne and sipped it, looking around.

'What are you thinking?' Luke's voice was for her ears only.

'That it looks like a film set,' she said without thinking.

Irony tinged his smile. 'With us as the extras?'

She nodded. 'It's so…everything's *right*. It's like a romantic fantasy.'

'Good,' he said. 'The committee who organised it worked extremely hard to make it exactly that. Our table's over here.'

The band struck up and the MC walked into the centre of the empty dance floor and welcomed them, telling them of the amazing amount of money the evening had earned. Everyone cheered and clapped, and then the MC announced the first dance, making a wry comment about the difference between old Europe where the tune was composed and this tropical paradise.

Fleur kept her gaze fixed on the dance floor as the band swung into a waltz.

'May I have this dance?' Luke asked formally.

She tried for an airy tone, but to her dismay it came out tense and somewhat forced. 'Of course.'

Hand in the small of her back once again, he guided her onto the floor.

Fleur blessed the high school in New Zealand that had run dancing lessons before each midwinter ball; she wasn't an expert, but at least she knew how to waltz. Luke, however, possessed both the knowledge and that intangible something that translated into grace on the dance floor.

After a few seconds he murmured, 'We're supposed to be lovers—soon, if not already. I'm afraid you're not going to convince anyone if you persist in holding yourself a sedate three inches away from me.'

His smile was teasing, but his metallic eyes demanded her compliance. Reluctantly she forced herself to melt against him as his arm tightened around her waist. She kept her gaze on his white dress shirt and tried to relax, to ignore the sensuous shivers running through her as the movement of his lean, assured body worked an enchantment as old as time.

He turned his head so that his voice would reach her ears. At the soft heat of his breath on her earlobe she was assailed by a pang of sensation so sharp and fierce it shocked her into almost missing a step.

'I hope you're looking soulful,' he murmured.

She said in a brittle voice, 'I don't think I can quite manage soulful. Would languishing do?'

Amusement deepened his voice. 'No, too Victorian. You're not the languishing or soulful sort anyway. Perhaps we should just try talking to each other like sensible beings. Have you enjoyed the evening so far?'

Sensible? How could she mimic being sensible, when a divine recklessness was smashing through her inhibitions and barriers as though they were matchwood?

So she found him hugely attractive. According to the magazines, lots of other women did, too. Why should she be any different?

And accepting that she was just one of many didn't mean she had to surrender to this tantalising expectancy. She had little enough experience, but she wasn't stupid; women as well as men could desire without wanting any sort of relationship. She'd only known Luke for a few days—far too early to form any sort of attachment.

Wrap this fierce, uncontrollable response up as prettily as you might—call it desire, fascination, need—but it was only packaging, the longing for closeness and commitment just another manifestation of hormones.

She could cope with it.

CHAPTER EIGHT

'I'M ENJOYING the evening very much,' Fleur said sedately. 'I think it's a great way to raise money for charity. Everyone seems to be having a wonderful time.'

Luke's arm flexed as they swung around in an elegant pivot that brought her even closer to him. Another feverish shiver drove every thought from her head.

'I don't think sensible is the right word to use for us at the moment,' he said thoughtfully, as though they were discussing some matter of politics.

The hand in the small of her back moved a few inches lower, holding her against him so that she felt every movement of his big, lean body.

Still with that considering inflection, he went on, 'Stimulated might be the right word, or perhaps aware—extremely aware. Your hand's trembling.'

Fleur swallowed to ease her dry throat and looked

at the hand on his upper arm. It was clenching, and the muscles beneath were like iron.

She forced her fingers straight on the white sleeve of his jacket and said thinly, 'I'm scared.'

'What of?' This time his voice was cold and sure and very formidable. 'You're completely safe, Fleur.'

'From—this?'

He didn't pretend not to know what she was talking about. 'Yes,' he said crisply. 'I don't go in for casual affairs and I despise people who do. I'm attracted to you, but you've made it quite obvious that although you feel the same way you don't want to act on it. That's fine.'

She should have been relieved instead of feeling let down. Collecting her thoughts, she said, 'I didn't think you were going to leap on me or anything, but…'

'You wondered,' he supplied when she dried up, her tongue tangling with the words as she realised where her thoughts were tending. 'You don't strike me as being very experienced. Or could it be that you've had some bad experiences?'

'No,' she said uneasily. Apart from the usual high school crushes, she'd had no experience at all.

She closed her mouth with a determination that came close to a snap. Until instinct leaped into the breach and warned her that such frankness might be dangerous, she'd been about to admit that she'd never felt like this before. She went on clumsily, 'I do trust you.'

'I'm glad. Trust me further, and rest your head on my chest,' he said, and when she obeyed, he lowered his head so that his breath fanned across her skin. 'Nobody can see what we're talking about, and it looks good.'

Fleur almost cringed. Here she was, afire with dangerous, forbidden need, yet he was so controlled he could talk about how they appeared to onlookers.

She caught the flash of a bulb. 'I didn't realise there'd be photographers here.'

'Some people like being in magazines,' he said aloofly, his tone revealing he wasn't one of them.

Surprised, she watched a woman working the crowd while Luke said, 'She has strict instructions. No shots of anyone dancing, and permission has to be given first. And the magazine is donating a hefty sum to the charity.'

'So everyone wins. From your tone, I gather you didn't want them here.'

'They leave a nasty taste in my mouth. I've been stung too many times by magazines that use innuendo and gossip to sell copies. Apparently people actually believe what they print,' he said, each word edged with contempt. 'If I'd bedded as many women as I've been linked with I'd be dead of exhaustion by now. Apart from anything else, I'm too busy.'

'So you won't be selling the rights to your wedding to one of them,' she said.

'Believe it. When I get married it will be here, where I can control the exposure.' He paused, then said, 'And when I decide to marry I want what my parents have— a good marriage based on complete trust.'

'You're lucky,' she said bleakly, trying to ignore the surge of pleasure building deep inside her, insidious as a fire smouldering beneath the earth. 'My parents taught me that marriages fall apart and that children can be used as weapons.'

Luke lifted his head and looked down at her bright crown of hair. Her dossier had been brief; she'd led a blameless, rather constricted life after her parents had divorced. Money had been scarce as her father had skipped to Australia to avoid paying support. The bitter parting was probably the reason she'd had no relationships in her year at university. Looking after her invalid mother meant that she'd had no time for any since then.

Was she a virgin?

A pang of fierce desire tightened his body. Hell, he thought disgustedly, he was turning into a satyr. He'd always steered clear of innocents, preferring lovers who were satisfied with what they were getting— fidelity as long as the relationship lasted, generosity and good sex. Most of them were still friends.

'That's tough,' he said quietly. 'Divorce is bad

enough, but kids need to know they mean more to their parents than convenient weapons.'

'I'm over it now. Tell me, who is Janna? I asked before, but you managed to avoid answering.'

Luke thought of the message he'd been handed as they left the house. 'She's an old friend,' he said, 'who happens to have hair the same colour as yours, only hers isn't natural.'

She looked at him with raised brows and a hint of mockery that gave her green eyes a swift, inviting feline quality. 'What makes you think mine is?'

'The fact that you blush so easily.' Sure enough, her magnificent cheekbones heated under his amused scrutiny.

'You know it's the bane of my life,' she said ruefully. 'Were you expecting her to visit you? Is that why the man took me to your house when I fainted in front of the car?'

He shook his head. 'Collapsed. And, no, I wasn't expecting her.'

'But?'

Luke settled for telling her as little as possible. 'But nothing. There's a superficial resemblance, which is why my driver—who'd never seen her in the flesh—thought you were her. However, he'd have picked you up and brought you home anyway.'

'Does everything that happens on Fala'isi land on your doorstep?'

'Not when my father's here,' he said evenly.

She'd become rigid again, holding herself away from him, and he was surprised at the irritation he felt at her subtle withdrawal.

Deliberately he drew her close, smiling down into her face, his lashes drooping so that only she could see the determination in his eyes. She stiffened a second, then relaxed, her slender body pliant in his arms.

She felt strangely right there, he thought, nodding to Guy Bagaton across the dance floor.

Fleur was fighting back a pang of frighteningly bitter jealousy. Just what was his relationship to this Janna person? Past lovers? Almost certainly.

She followed him through a particularly complex manoeuvre, then the music wound up to a triumphant conclusion, and everyone clapped and began to leave the floor.

After that Fleur danced with the other men of their party, sat out the energetic ones with the Princess—who was amusing, interesting company—and shared more dances with Luke, where they playacted for everyone to see. She pretended not to watch when Luke danced with Gabrielle, but she realised that Luke had been right; the girl was definitely possessive about him.

A little later she came across Fleur in the ladies' room and said graciously, 'I hope you are enjoying yourself.'

'Very much,' Fleur replied with a smile.

Gabrielle looked at her with raised brows. 'You are not his usual sort of woman.' She flashed a smile that was close to feline. 'Do you realise he is using you?'

Unprepared for such an open attack, Fleur turned on the tap and let cold water play over her wrists. 'My relationship with Luke is nobody's business but ours.'

Gabrielle stiffened. 'You are wrong. I am telling you this because I like you, but if you are hoping that this liaison is more than a temporary fling you will be wrong, because eventually he and I are to be married. Did you know that?'

How on earth did she deal with this? Fleur said, 'Do you really think Luke would flaunt a lover in front of the woman he's engaged to?'

The younger woman sketched a very Gallic shrug. 'You are a romantic, so naturally you don't understand our way of conducting marriages. This has been decided for ever—it is a matter of honour to both families, and of course there is a lot of money tied up in it, too. My dowry will be my grandfather's business interests—Luke is already in charge of them, but when we marry they will become his. Luke is more French than English in his attitude towards such things.'

Fleur turned off the tap and said neutrally into the silence, 'It sounds very pragmatic.'

It also sounded very possible. Luke hadn't mentioned anything about business interests when he'd persuaded her into this charade. And she'd agreed to it without thought—because she trusted him.

No, she thought, her mind working furiously. Why on earth would he have suggested the masquerade if he planned to eventually marry Gabrielle and her inheritance? It would make him a horrible man...

Perhaps he was.

Gabrielle finished applying lipstick and smiled. 'We are a pragmatic race. But it will be a good marriage, and there will be no divorce. Our children will have a happy home life. Of course he will probably always enjoy chasing little redheads and, yes, I will mind a little, although I will always know that such adventures mean nothing. You have no chance of marrying him. He is a Chapman; his great-grandmother was descended from the old aristocracy of France. He knows what is due his position.'

And it's not some insignificant New Zealander with no family and no money, her tone implied.

Fleur bristled, but to her great relief the Princess's arrival put an end to the conversation. Nevertheless, it left Fleur with a nasty taste, especially when she saw Gabrielle flirting skilfully with the film star as they danced. She certainly didn't look as though her heart was touched by Luke's supposed betrayal.

Apart from that the evening was an enchantment. Fleur looked around thinking wryly that no cliché had been forgotten; the moon shone with unadulterated glory over the island, rollers crashed onto the reef with muted thunder and the perfumes of the tropics suffused the soft night air.

Supper was served on the beach, a magnificent spread of local and imported foods, champagne flowed, and after supper a group of Fala'isian young people danced for them—starting with a war challenge done with flaming torches, and ending in a wild, erotic hula that sent a buzz of interest through the guests.

Heated applause followed the entertainers as they undulated into the darkness, and then the band struck up again, and Luke held out his hand to Fleur. 'What do you think of our dancers?'

'They are gorgeous—and they dance brilliantly.' She moved into his arms with more confidence now. The lights had dimmed, and around them people were drifting into slow easy steps. 'The challenge was great, and the hula was superb.'

'You understand Maori, I gather?' At her surprised glance he expanded, 'I think you and Guy were probably the only other off-islanders who realised the show was a parody, a camped-up version of what tourists expect to see. I saw you laugh at one place.'

'I have a working knowledge of Maori, and although there are substantial differences between that and Fala'isian I can sort of pick up the gist of a conversation as I go along. So, yes, I got some of the allusions. Can you speak it?'

'Of course.' He sounded surprised. 'My sisters and I grew up speaking three languages—French with our great-grandmother, the local tongue with everyone else, and English with our parents.'

'You were fortunate.'

His wide shoulder lifted in a shrug beneath her hand. 'Children learn languages quickly. According to my mother, the trick is to make sure they stick to one at a time. When my sisters and I were small we used to speak a mixture of all three until my parents made quite strict rules. If you started a conversation in one, you had to keep to it and finish it in that language. It made life simpler.'

'You have two sisters, don't you?'

He didn't exactly pause, but she had the feeling he didn't want to talk about his sisters. 'Yes, one older and one younger than me.'

'Do they live here?'

'One's in Paris and the other in New York at the moment.'

Rebuffed, she said lightly, 'I'd have loved siblings.'

'We get on well,' he said.

Fleur envied him that simple, confident assertion.

He steered the subject away from his sisters. 'I understood you to say that your father has another family in Australia.'

'I don't even know where they are,' she told him. 'When my parents broke up my father told me that if I didn't go with him I'd never see him again. I stayed with my mother, so that was it. The only reason I know about his other child is that when the divorce came through he wrote to tell my mother that he and his new partner had already had a son.'

Luke's mouth hardened. 'Do you have any other relatives—cousins?'

'In England,' she said evenly. 'We exchange Christmas cards.'

He hugged her, a swift contraction of his arms with no sexual implication at all. Oddly touched by his swift response, she smiled mistily up at him. Luke had everything—money, power, a family he loved, outstanding physical attributes, yet he had enough empathy to understand how very lonely it could be sometimes when you had no one.

Fleur felt a quiver in the air—as though something deep and basic had changed between them. His gaze dropped to her mouth and darkened, then flicked up to hold hers. For several seconds they danced slowly and more slowly, until a raucous male voice broke the spell.

'Hey, Luke, mate, get off the floor if you don't want to dance.' A tall, balding man grinned openly as both Luke's and Fleur's heads swung around.

Heat burned Fleur's cheeks. The man's partner

waved at them, her smile sympathetic and slightly envious, and Luke laughed quietly and pulled Fleur close to him, guiding her away.

After a few seconds he said, 'Time to go home, I think.'

Fleur nodded. 'The Princess will be pleased.' Yes, that was fine—her voice was cool and colourless. 'She's looking a bit tired, and she hasn't got up for the last two dances.'

He gave her another sharp look, but didn't hold it. 'She's probably a bit jet-lagged.'

Sure enough, no one objected to the idea of leaving, though Gabrielle gave the film star a regretful glance or two when she and her grandfather got into the second car, driven by a chauffeur.

Luke drove through the silent night. No one said much as the road wound beneath palm groves by the sea, and then over a spur of the central mountain range and down into the bay where Luke's house sprawled in its exotic garden.

Fleur gazed blindly into the moonlight, every sense alert and tense with a useless anticipation that wouldn't be squelched, however hard she tried.

Because Luke wasn't going to make love to her—not with a house full of guests.

'Tired?' His voice broke into the silence.

'A bit,' she admitted. 'It's been fabulous in the true sense of the word—like something out of a fairytale.' Only the princes in those fables were a bloodless lot, not like Luke.

'I've enjoyed it, too.'

Casual words, the sort of thing he probably said after any social occasion, yet she hugged them to her heart.

Back at the house the Prince and Princess went to their room. Fleur waited with Luke only until the second car disgorged its passengers, then said her goodnights.

Once in her bedroom, she went across to the dressing table and glanced sideways at her reflection. She looked reckless, she thought warily—all green mysterious eyes and a sultry, beckoning mouth. The cosmetics experts certainly knew their stuff!

And then her eyes fell onto the fabulous pearl pendant Luke had lent her.

Biting her lip, she slipped it over her head, hesitating for a second with it in her hand. The gold and diamonds glinted coldly, but the pearl lay warm in her palm, its lustre as beckoning as the moon.

Another memory, she thought sadly.

She didn't want the lovely, precious thing in her room overnight; the responsibility was too much. Holding the pendant carefully, she opened her door and saw Luke and the Prince talking down the other end of the corridor.

Although she'd been quiet, the men turned the

instant she appeared. She swallowed, because on both dark faces there was the same look—intent, almost predatory, as though two warriors were conferring on tactics.

After a final low-voiced comment to the Prince, Luke strode towards her while Guy Bagaton went into the bedroom he shared with his wife.

Luke kept his eyes on her while they walked towards each other. He wasn't frowning, but something in that keen, burnished gaze intensified the aura of determination surrounding him, and she shivered in spite of the warmth.

As he came up she held out the pendant. 'You'd better lock it up.'

He took it from her, his eyes scanning her face. 'All right?'

'Yes,' she said abruptly.

She stepped back and closed the door, wondering bleakly if any other woman had ever shut the door in his face. Probably not, she thought starkly, pulling the lovely silk dress over her head. Like all the other clothes, she'd leave it behind when she left Fala'isi.

She was just coming out of the bathroom when her door opened again, and Luke came in, moving with the noiseless, predatory gait of some big animal. When he saw her, he stopped, and the door swung closed behind him.

'I did knock,' he said abruptly. 'I didn't realise you were in the shower.'

Shocked into silence, Fleur watched him with enormous eyes. Against Luke's black and white splendour she felt very undressed in the camisole and matching shorts she wore to bed, and very vulnerable, too, she thought with painful honesty, a pulse beating rapidly in her throat. She looked around for her wrap, but it was in the wardrobe and she wasn't going to walk across there in her flimsy garments.

Luke said curtly, 'We need to talk.'

She swallowed. 'About what?'

'Something that's come up.' His mouth compressed. 'Where's your dressing gown?'

'In the wardrobe. Shut your eyes.'

Shrugging, he obeyed, and she scuttled across the room to the wardrobe and pulled on the crisp cotton dressing gown. Tying the belt around her waist she said, 'Is this about Gabrielle?'

Luke's opened eyes were uncomfortably penetrating. 'Why?'

'Because if it is I think you should know what she said to me this evening.'

Luke's frown deepened while she hastily sketched in the substance of the conversation. When she'd finished he said without inflection, 'I wonder if that's what her grandfather's told her.'

'Is it true?'

Her heart picked up speed while she waited for his answer.

But when it came it wasn't exactly comforting. 'I bought everything from him two years ago.'

He went on with harsh distinctness, 'He didn't sell his interests to me as a sweetener for a marriage deal. It was a purely business decision, because he has nobody else to leave them to—Gabrielle's father died young, and Gabrielle herself is more artistic than businesslike. He did suggest marriage in the early stages, but I told him I wasn't interested.'

Pushing her hair back from her face, Fleur asked, 'Then why does Gabrielle believe that she's as good as engaged to you?' Too late, she realised she sounded like a jealous woman and tried to temper her question with a swift addition. 'I think she really believes that, Luke. I don't know her, of course, but either it's her own fantasy she's convinced will come true, or it's something she's been told.'

'Not by me.' Luke's tone poured scorn on any such suggestion. 'I've just endured a somewhat embarrassing attempt on her part to seduce me.'

Appalled by a violent desire to pull the French girl's hair out then send her packing, Fleur said woodenly, 'I see.'

He frowned. 'I didn't realise things had gone this far. They're leaving tomorrow morning, with Lauren and Guy, but I'll deal with the situation before they go.'

'How?'

He glanced across at her. 'First of all, I'll spend the night in here,' he said evenly, his tone daring her to object. 'That will convince her grandfather, if not her, that she has no hope. He's a man of the old school, and he'll know that I wouldn't flaunt a mistress in his face if I were planning to marry his granddaughter.'

Fleur's stomach dropped in a mixture of head-strong excitement and fear as she scanned his flinty, implacable face. He didn't say it, but he didn't need to; she had no choice. Whatever, she'd find herself sharing a room.

She fought back a bubble of anticipation, bright and fragile and eager, and demanded, 'And will he be able to convince her she has no hope?'

'I imagine so. I've already made it more than clear to her that I play no part in her future. Before they leave tomorrow I'll make sure her grandfather understands this, too.'

A shiver ran through Fleur at his tone—cold and utterly ruthless. Yet, in the long run, wouldn't it be crueller not to do what was necessary to squelch Gabrielle's forlorn fantasy?

Making a final stand, she said, 'She told me she wouldn't care if you still chased redheads.'

'Did she?' he returned, his tone frigid. 'I find that damned insulting. When I marry I want a wife who loves me enough to be jealous.'

Surrendering, Fleur said bitterly, 'Heaven preserve me from dominating men!'

'And me from recalcitrant women.' He allowed a gleam of amusement to appear in his eyes. 'Take off your wrap and get into bed. Don't worry, I won't take advantage of the opportunity. I prefer my women willing.'

Oh, she was willing enough, but not—not like this, she thought confusedly. She tried one last time. 'How will she know that you've spent the night here?'

His brow lifted in sardonic amusement. 'I'm prepared to bet that within twenty minutes there'll be a tap on the door and she'll be there, ready to ask charmingly for something feminine she's neglected to pack. Now, just in case she comes sooner rather than later, get into bed.'

She obeyed, wondering how on earth she'd let herself get into this pickle.

But when she hauled the covers up, she realised he was coming towards her. Fleur froze, watching him with eyes that grew wider and wider. Surely he wasn't… No…

But he kept on coming. When he pulled back the bedclothes on the other side of the bed she bolted up and said furiously, 'You said you wouldn't—'

'And I'll keep that promise,' he said between strong white teeth, obviously thoroughly fed up, 'but if Gabrielle arrives I need to establish that I've actually been in this bed with you. It would be better, of course, if the bedclothes were in tatters across the floor and you and I were lying in naked abandon in each other's arms, but somehow I don't see that happening, do you?'

CHAPTER NINE

COLOUR scorched Fleur's skin. She could have shrunk into a heap of embarrassment, but an angry pride kept her upright.

'No, I thought not,' Luke said, with a silky distinctness that sent a shiver running the length of her spine. He sounded dangerous, and she didn't blame him.

After all, none of this was his fault, just as it wasn't hers.

He went on sardonically, 'So if you feel you'll be contaminated by being in a bed with me—even with my clothes still on—you'd better get out for the five or ten seconds it's going to take me to rumple the pillow and the sheets.'

'Oh, all right!' Humiliated, she scrambled out, snatching up her wrap to sling around her shoulders.

From beneath her lashes she watched him lower himself into the bed and stretch out full length, her throat drying at the easy litheness of his big body beneath the white shirt and narrow black trousers.

Lord, but he was *big!* Even dancing with him hadn't prepared her for the sheer physical impact of him. Little needles of sensation tingled through her and she felt a suspicious meltdown of electricity at the junction of her thighs.

He moved his dark head on the pillows, making sure there was an indentation.

Dragging her mind away from the startling, exciting contrast of his black hair on the white pillows, Fleur said with a twisted smile, 'It's just as well you know more about this sort of thing than I do.'

'Sex?' He registered her slight start with a cynical smile.

'Yes,' she said on a snap.

He didn't say anything more, and the silence dragged, became taut and filled with unspoken words and emotions.

Finally he got out and looked down at the impression left by his body. 'All right, you can get back in now,' he said, and strode with that swift, noiseless panther stride across to the window.

Fleur scurried back into the bed, but the linen sheets carried the faint, earthy scent of his natural odour, a sexy hint to women that indicated his strength and his potency.

'What happens now?' she asked, carefully not looking at the side of the room that held him. The corners of her eyes caught movement; she suspected he was taking off his clothes. A wave of hot desire clutched her low down in the pit of her stomach, making her move uneasily.

'I'll strip off and lie down on the sofa. Don't worry, it won't be long before she comes.'

'You seem to know an awful lot about Gabrielle if you're so sure she'll do this.'

His laugh was low and cynical. 'I know a fair amount about women, yes. When she knocks I'll come across and get in beside you.'

Her heart jumped in her chest.

She wondered if he could hear her breathing, and lay concentrating on breathing slowly and steadily. He didn't stir. He'd probably gone to sleep, she thought crossly.

She wished he'd snore. Snoring would make him ordinary. You couldn't possibly get into a lather over a man who snored.

Frowning she tried to think of home and what she was planning to do when she got back, but New Zealand seemed so far away, so thin and insubstantial, and her mind slipped into forbidden pathways.

What sort of lover was Luke? She wiped the ironic grimace from her lips. Superb, of course.

She suddenly thought of something and sat up. 'Luke, what about…?'

The words evaporated from her brain, because he instantly switched on the light and got to his feet.

The swift blossoming of the lamp spread a wash of golden light over the powerful muscles and sleek skin of his shoulders. Heat robbed Fleur of coherent thought. Dry-mouthed and dazzled, she noted the pattern of hair across his bare bronze torso.

'What about…?' he prompted brusquely.

A knock on the door jolted them both into silence. Heart pumping madly, she stared at the uncompromising determination of his face, and gasped when he picked up his shirt and tossed it on the floor beside the bed.

He took three strides and hauled her into his arms, kissing her with a passion that set her pulse rate soaring into the stratosphere.

Then he fell back onto the bed with her, knocking a pillow onto the floor.

He was half over her, kissing her passionately, when the door opened.

'I am so sorry, but—' Gabrielle's voice stopped.

Luke lifted his head and gazed at her, then got to his feet in magnificent, half-naked authority. 'What is it?' he asked. And when she said nothing, he demanded bluntly, 'Is something the matter, Gabrielle? Your grandfather?'

Fleur sat up on the bed, and the intruder's stormy gaze went from Luke's handsome, controlled face to Fleur's—flushed, embarrassed and very obviously seriously kissed.

She had to admire the girl's composure, although her next words shocked her.

'Slut! Whore!' Gabrielle hissed, and started a low, fierce tirade in French.

Immediately Luke silenced her, his voice swift and cutting as the crack of a whip. 'I won't ask why you feel entitled to walk into someone else's room without invitation, but I'm telling you to go.'

Gabrielle's face crumpled, her veneer of sophistication fading to reveal her youth. She said unevenly, 'I am sorry. I just wanted to…'

With disciplined, formidable force, Luke said, 'I don't know how you developed the idea that there was some connection between us, but I want it stopped right now. When the time comes I will choose my own wife. Do you understand me?'

The girl nodded and repeated, 'I am sorry.'

'No more interviews with magazines hinting at a secret engagement, and no more sly tips to gossip columnists.'

Colour flooded Gabrielle's face. 'No,' she whispered. 'No more,' and, gulping, she turned and fled.

Fleur didn't blame her. Luke in a temper—even one so well controlled as this—was a truly daunting experience. But she couldn't let her go like that, and bolted off the bed.

'Don't follow her,' Luke said, closing the door, his expression rueful. 'I feel like someone who's just pulled the wings off a butterfly, but she'll need time to herself, not with you.'

'Perhaps the Princess—?' Fleur suggested tentatively.

His brows shot up. 'Your compassion is misplaced, I suspect. No, Lauren is probably sound asleep by now. Anyway, for all her flaws Gabrielle has guts and pride. I think she'd rather deal with this herself. Wouldn't you?'

Fleur shivered. 'Yes,' she admitted. 'I'm older than she is, though.'

'Probably not as experienced.' He looked down at her, his expression aloof. 'I'm sorry you had to endure that. I know I was cruel, but I needed to establish once and for all that she's been spinning moonbeams.'

'It's all right,' she said awkwardly.

He was too close. Adrenalin was still surging through her veins, and the subtle scent of aroused male was doing something weird to her thought processes—to say nothing of the remembered imprint of his mouth on hers and the weight of his body.

'When I asked you to do this I hoped I was anticipating something that might not even exist,' he said. 'I had no idea it was already such a problem, or that she'd be so persistent.'

'Do you think you've scotched it?'

He shrugged, the light gleaming on his wide

shoulders, tanned and sleek and eminently touchable. Fleur's fingertips tingled, and only a massive exercise of will stopped her from leaning the few inches between them and pressing her mouth to his skin, drawing him back down onto the bed with her so they could finish what they'd started…

'I hope so. I'll talk to her grandfather tomorrow in case he's been feeding her these ideas.'

She nodded and stared straight ahead. 'Right. Now, as that's done, you might as well go back to your own room,' she said brightly, the brittle words almost shattering as she articulated them.

'Sorry,' he said coolly. 'But just in case, I'm staying here.'

She swung around, eyes enormous in her flushed face, her breasts heaving beneath the fragile camisole top. 'No!' she said explosively. 'I don't want you—'

He was watching her with narrowed, intent eyes, but he interrupted with a smile that was half scorn, half hunger. 'Don't lie to me, Fleur,' he said. 'You're scared, but you want me all right. Just as I want you.'

He trailed a lean fingertip along her collarbone, letting it linger as he watched the shifting expressions on her face, the swift fear replaced by a slow dawning of desire mirrored in her green eyes and the soft curves of her lush mouth.

'Whoever named you Fleur should have chosen Margaret,' he said, his voice deep and barely controlled. 'It means pearl, and you were born to wear them. Your skin is more beautiful than the pearl you wore tonight, because it's warm and fine and smooth as silk. Did you know pearls fade and die if they're not worn?'

She dragged a breath into her lungs, and Luke had to concentrate on her mouth, her eyes, so that he didn't get driven astray by the soft curves beneath the flimsy camisole.

'No,' she whispered. 'Do they?'

'They need to be caressed and oiled and loved by their owners.'

He shouldn't be doing this. He should stop the slow wooing with words, the silken caress, the heated, desperate appetite that had been a constant companion since the moment he'd seen her.

Luke had never made love to a woman who hadn't made it obvious that she wanted sex with him. Always he'd steered clear of virgins and the inexperienced, but something stronger than caution and respect drove him now, a raw hunger that undermined his self-control.

It took every ounce of will to close his eyes and say, 'Tell me to leave.'

She was silent and still for so long he opened his eyes. Seeing the struggle in her expression, he said on a raw note, 'It's all right. I had no right to put the responsibility onto you.'

'If I said go, would you?' she asked.

He said, 'Yes.'

Fleur was silent again, then she nodded, a single firm inclination of her head. 'I want you to stay,' she said, and leaned forward to press a kiss over his heart, potent as a spell, sweet as love, fiery as torment.

Luke froze, then lifted her face with a hand around her chin and examined her with metallic, relentless eyes. When he spoke the word slipped between thin, barely moving lips. 'Sure?'

Fleur felt that unsparing survey like a blow, but she'd made up her mind. Whatever happened she knew she wanted this one night with him. 'Utterly and completely sure,' she said on a whisper that came too close to a vow.

For several searing seconds longer he held her gaze, his smile fading. Then he bent his head, and with a noiseless sigh Fleur yielded to his demanding kiss, her arms creeping up to embrace him, heart and soul yielding to a desire that would last for the rest of her life.

Still kissing, he lifted her and carried her across to the bed. 'Take off that flimsy little piece of satin,' he commanded in a deep, husky voice.

She slipped the camisole top over her head, and he let her slide down his lean body so that she felt the glory of her skin against his. Fire rippled through her, burning away everything but a need so keen and pure that she groaned with the immensity of it. Her body clamoured for him, for the release only he could give her.

The future meant nothing; she couldn't think of anything but the now, with Luke making slow, measured love to her, using his skills and knowledge to summon amazingly erotic sensations from a source deep inside her. Shivering, gasping, she ran her hands across his shoulders, exulting in the most primitive way when the muscles beneath his skin flexed and coiled beneath her palms.

He wooed her with kisses, trailing them down her throat to settle over the passionate hollow there, then up to her earlobe where she discovered a new pleasure, a thrilling arrow of excitement at the touch of his teeth that arrowed to the centre of her being.

'All right?' He asked it with a smile, because he knew.

All right? Everything was so right that she thought she might die from the rapture of how astonishingly all right it was.

Smiling at him, she traced his mouth with a tentative fingertip. 'Magnificently all right,' she said in a husky voice that didn't sound like her.

He laughed deep in his throat, and kissed her again, then lifted her again and put her on the bed, this time taking her by surprise when his mouth found the soft swell of one breast. Heat fountained through her, fierce and urgent and hungry. She arched into his taut body, frantically seeking something further, something more, and he cupped her pleading breast in one lean hand.

'Look,' he said.

Blushing furiously, she obeyed; dark skin against pale, his powerful hand against her soft curves, the implicit contrast between male and female, nurturer and protector, two entirely different yet complementary strengths. As she watched, feeling like a deliciously aroused voyeur, her breasts tightened and the nipples stood up like small insistent peaks, sending a sensual charge through her that intoxicated every cell in her body.

'Edgar Rice Burroughs probably said it best,' Luke said, an undertone of wry humour in his voice, 'when he wrote, "Me Tarzan, you Jane". The irresistible age-old lure of the opposite…'

His mouth settled around the tip of her breast. All the strength fled Fleur's body. Racked by delicious shivers, she sagged against him, her eyes closing against the unbelievable pleasure his seeking mouth gave her.

Fleur had wondered what making love was really like. After listening to less than rapturous descriptions from her friends, she'd decided that although desire was clearly a powerful force, the actual act itself was more earthy, more prosaic.

How totally, joylessly wrong she'd been! Her untried body reacted to Luke's caresses with a lack of inhibition that might shock her later, but now seemed the only possible and fitting response. Eagerly she followed where he led, mimicked his caresses with her own, followed the dictates of her own needs.

And her heart.

Luke's arms around her, his magic hands working enchantments on her, his voice strained with the effort to control his hunger, all combined to lift her into another plane of existence. Her only fear was that when the time came she'd disappoint him.

And even that worry vanished when at last he found that sensitive, vulnerable spot between her legs. Transfixed by a craving so potent it shook her whole body, Fleur cried out and arched into him, hands clutching, her mouth seeking as she kissed his throat.

'Sweetheart,' he rasped, the cords of his neck standing out with the effort it took to control his hunger, 'don't be so... God, what am I saying? Let me pace us, OK?'

Wild-eyed, she stared at him. 'Pace?'

'Trust me?' he said, with a quirk of his lips more like desperation than amusement.

After a moment she nodded, reassured somehow by the fact that he was clearly as close to that elusive fulfilment as she was.

'Then, however much you despise the idea, can

you just let me do the work for a little while?' He must have noticed her bewilderment because he kissed her hard and fast and said against her lips, 'If you touch me I'm not going to be any good to you for quite some time.'

Blushing scarlet, she nodded, and he said on a note of laughing astonishment, 'I didn't know you coloured all over.'

And he traced the progress of her blush with his mouth until Fleur gave up thinking and abandoned herself to rapture and mounting eagerness.

Even when he explored her with his hand, finding the small spot that kicked her passion into even higher gear, she managed to contain her urge to press herself against him. Her body tensed; sensation piled upon sensation, coalesced into waves of consuming delight that surged higher and higher through her, until they climaxed in a torrent of overwhelming ecstasy.

Shuddering with its force, she went limp, and turned her face into his shoulder. He stroked her, long gentle sweeps of his hand from her shoulder to her thigh, and she could feel the urgent prod of his penis against her.

After a few moments she lifted a bemused face to his searching hooded steel-grey eyes. 'That was wonderful,' she said in a troubled voice, 'but what about you?'

'Sometimes it hurts the first time. I wanted you to feel pleasure first.'

When he released her and turned away she had to stop her plea with her hand. He sat up and she realised that he was searching in the pocket of his trousers.

Understanding flooded her. She watched the lamplight play over the sleek body she had explored with her own tentative caresses as he donned protection. Half of her was relieved, the other half fiercely condemned the need.

Bearing Luke's baby would be heaven...

He came back down and looped his arms around her, pulling her against the length of his body so that she could feel his desire. His face was drawn, the arrogant framework more pronounced than it had been.

I've done that to him, she thought dreamily.

Her colour deepened, but she held his gaze. 'How did you know it would be the first time for me?' And at his smile she muttered, 'Damned blushes!'

He laughed at that. 'Even without that, your innocence proclaims itself. And I like your blushes very much.'

He kissed her again, deepening the sensuous exploration until she sighed into his mouth and moulded herself against him. Astonished, she felt desire stir once more, but nothing, she was sure, could possibly be as good as that initial rapture.

Luke wooed her with caresses that slowly became bolder and bolder, until she gasped when he eased his fingers inside her, setting off a firestorm that almost convulsed her again in another addictive climax.

In a voice that was rough and exciting, he said, 'This might hurt.'

'I don't care,' she moaned, hips jerking against him, her hands pulling him even closer.

He took her with one powerful thrust, forcing his way past the fragile barrier. She froze, waiting for pain. It came, but briefly, and fled without aftershocks.

Bodies linked, Luke lifted her chin and asked harshly, 'All right?'

The colour in two bright spots on her cheekbones almost matched the fire in her green eyes. 'We've had this conversation already. If it was any *more* all right,' she muttered, glaring at him, 'I might just die of it.'

Luke caught back the laughter that threatened, losing it to a tide of sexual longing so ardent that his next movements took him utterly by surprise. Tossing hard-won restraint to the winds, he withdrew swiftly and then thrust again, instinct telling him that long and slow wasn't necessary.

Her ragged cry caught in her throat; he felt her hands clench into fists on his hips, and then all sensible thought vanished as his control snapped and he took her without finesse, without anything but raw passion and the need to make this woman entirely his.

Fleur shuddered in ecstasy, so lost to the moment that she had no idea where she was for long minutes until the sensations ebbed, leaving her sweat-washed and boneless with exhaustion, still savouring the acute pleasure of meeting heaven in Luke's arms.

An aching sadness crept through her. She was under no illusions. This, she knew, didn't mean anything as much to him as it did to her.

When he lifted himself onto his elbows she made a soft sound of regret, of protest, but he ignored it and turned on his side, scooping her over to lie half on top of him. His arms kept the faint chill of rejection at bay. She listened to the heavy thud of his heart, her own in synch as they slowed down and resumed normal speed.

Voice rumbling against her ear, he said, 'No pain, I assume?'

'None worth mentioning,' she said, yawning. Her voice slurred the words. She yawned again, and said more precisely, 'I didn't think that could happen— the first time. I read somewhere that it takes two years for most women to trust a man enough to have an orgasm with him.'

Her voice trailed away on the last words.

Luke said, 'Tell me about it tomorrow. Sleep now.'

He moved slightly, the light went off, and she fell immediately into sleep so deep that it took Luke's voice to wake her.

Shocked and disoriented, she stared at the ceiling. Her first thought was that Gabrielle had once again intruded, but when she lurched up on her elbow and stared at him she saw he was talking into a mobile phone.

And he was furious, she thought, her body tightening as though anticipating a threat. Splendidly naked, the light from the lamp shining over him in slabs of copper and gold, he was standing, black brows drawn together in a frown that sent a shiver through her.

'Are you sure?' he demanded. A few seconds later he said explosively, 'Damn it all to hell!'

Chilled, she sat up, hauling the sheet to cover her naked breasts when she saw his eyes follow the movement. He was listening intently, and his gaze flicked up to her face, scanning it as though she were a complete stranger.

'Do that,' he said, the words crisp and cold and forceful. 'I'll see to things this end.'

He snapped the telephone closed and said, 'I have a problem, and you're going back to New Zealand.'

'What—what do you mean?' she asked, her heart plummeting in her chest. No sign of the tender lover now; he was looking at her with an icy, impersonal gaze that struck down every foolish, inchoate hope.

'Get dressed. I'll explain on the way to the airport.'

Fleur pressed trembling lips together. 'All right,' she said, but didn't move.

He said impatiently, 'Get up, Fleur.'

'Not with you looking,' she muttered.

His brows shot up. 'It's too late for regrets,' he said curtly. 'You don't have time for them, anyway. I want you off the island as quickly as possible.'

The mobile phone rang again. He flicked it open and turned away, and Fleur unfroze for long enough to swing her legs out of the bed.

In shattered silence she collected a change of clothes and retired to the bathroom. Swiftly, holding herself together with a kind of dull resignation, she showered before changing into trousers and a shirt.

When she emerged Luke had gone and the yawning housekeeper was packing her clothes.

Miraculously, Fleur didn't blush at the state of the wrecked bed. Instead she said, 'I won't be needing those. Just leave them, please.'

Susi said uncertainly, 'But Luke told me—'

Fleur shrugged. It seemed too much trouble to be worrying about clothes when Luke was sending her home. Nevertheless she said, 'I won't be taking them.'

Luke appeared in the door. 'Come and have something to eat and a cup of coffee,' he said coolly.

Startled, Fleur looked at the windows, but it was still dark outside. Although the thought of food made her feel sick, she could do with a charge of caffeine to help her get through the next few hours.

A tray was waiting in his study—sandwiches and

coffee. Mutely she refused the food, but drank the hot liquid, waiting for something to break through the shell of numbness that was building from her heart outwards.

Luke said, 'I'm sorry about this. I'm sending you back to New Zealand because an emergency has come up.'

She nodded, hoping he wouldn't go on making excuses. 'It's all right,' she said, forcing her tone to be brisk and unimpressed.

He frowned. 'It is not,' he said curtly. 'I don't want to send you away—and after what's just happened even less so.'

'Look,' she said desperately, 'let's just leave it at that, OK? What happened was great—no one could have had a better first time. Thank you.' She poured extra milk into the coffee to cool it and gulped more down, hoping the caffeine would jolt her brain into working again.

'I'm glad you think that way, but I'm not getting rid of you because we made love.' He stopped, then said in an uncompromising tone that meant business, 'Listen to me, Fleur, this is important. When you get to New Zealand my man will take you to my penthouse in Auckland, and I want you to stay there until I come and tell you that everything's clear.'

This command finally broke through her

numbness. 'You don't need to do that—I can find somewhere to stay.'

'I'm not offering you hospitality out of the kindness of my heart,' he said tautly.

'Then why?'

'Because you'll be safe there.'

Eyes enormous, she stared at him above the rim of the coffee cup. 'What on earth do you mean?'

CHAPTER TEN

LUKE had already worked out what to tell her. After a glance at his watch he poured himself another cup of coffee but left it on the table in front of him. Watching her he said bluntly, 'Because I've just been told that a man has got onto Fala'isi who quite possibly will try to kill you.'

She turned completely white, but that indomitable spirit held her upright, her gaze fixed with painful intensity on him. 'What?' she breathed. Then, before he had a chance to speak, she asked in a firmer voice, 'Why?'

Luke chose his words carefully. 'You wanted to know who Janna is. She was once a close friend; we parted, and six months ago she married. The day before you fainted so spectacularly in front of my car, she rang to tell me that she'd left her husband. According to her, he was convinced that she'd been carrying on an affair with me.'

Fleur's brain stopped. So did her breathing.

'And she said he had beaten her,' Luke concluded before ordering, 'Finish your coffee.'

Obediently she sipped, but she still felt cold and disoriented.

Luke went on, 'I didn't believe her. Or not entirely. She wanted my sympathy and my help, and she's prone to dramatising. However, I arranged for her to be taken to a safe house in Switzerland. When she flew to Paris instead I assumed she had been exaggerating. However, a couple of days after you began staying here she rang again. She'd flown into Fala'isi and hoped that I'd put her up.'

Janna didn't sound too bright, Fleur thought. Shivering, she said, 'Why? I mean—if he's convinced you're having an affair, by coming here she just reinforced his suspicions.'

He shrugged. 'She thought she'd covered her tracks, but it's damned near impossible to do that if the person chasing you has the resources to search you out.'

'Don't tell me,' Fleur said acidly, furious with the woman who'd put him in danger. 'Her husband has the resources.'

Luke lifted an ironic brow. 'He's a very rich man. I lodged her in a house my family own in the mountains. It's well-guarded and almost impossible to reach unless he hires a helicopter—which he won't be able to do. Unfortunately you look enough like her to fool anyone who doesn't know her very well.'

His words sent another chill scudding down her spine. 'So?'

'I assume that Janna's husband has discovered that someone of her appearance arrived in Fala'isi.' His voice was cool and level, but she discerned an intimidating note of flinty determination when he went on. 'And if he didn't already know, he'd certainly find out after conversations with one or two islanders that someone resembling Janna is living in my house and assumed to be my lover.'

'Is that why—am I a decoy?' she asked numbly.

Luke's face darkened. 'Hell, no!' he said explosively. 'Looking back, I should have taken more notice of Janna's story, but it seemed outrageous, and I thought she was trying to make him jealous by coming here. However, he's followed her, and as he landed here on a false passport and with a false name I have to assume that not only does he believe that you are her, but that he's up to no good.' He paused, before saying crisply, 'On the other hand he may merely be trying to avoid the paparazzi, who've finally worked out that they've separated and are trying to find out where they are.'

'Do you believe that?'

'No,' he said after a moment. 'Janna is terrified— utterly convinced that he'll try to kill her. Which is why you're going back to New Zealand.'

'Surely it would be better if I stay here so he can see that I'm not her—'

'No,' he interrupted decisively. 'This has nothing to do with you. You're going back to New Zealand, and I want your promise that you'll stay in my apartment until I give you the all-clear.'

She bit her lip. His steel-grey gaze demanded her agreement without compromise. And because she loved him, she said unevenly, 'Yes, of course I will. Does Janna think you're in any danger?'

His shoulders lifted in that swift shrug she'd always associate with him. 'She hasn't mentioned it. Anyway, I'm well protected.' He looked at her and said aloofly, 'But I want you well out of it.'

Fleur's whole being rose in tumultuous revolt, but she had no right to ask him to come to New Zealand with her. He wouldn't, anyway. He'd spent his life thinking of the people he'd one day be responsible for. That sense of obligation, of responsibility, had been bred in him, part of his heritage.

And once he had loved the other woman. Possibly he still did. Perhaps, she thought with a painful twist to her heart, she had merely been a substitute, a woman who looked like his true love.

She couldn't stop herself from asking, 'What are you going to do?'

He paused, his eyes hooded, then said deliberately, 'I think you'd be safer if you didn't know that.'

A squadron of chills rapidly followed the initial ones. Fleur took another gulp of coffee, but it failed to give her the warmth the first sip had produced.

Very carefully she drank the rest of it and set the cup down. 'You're really worried about her safety.' It wasn't a question.

'Yes, I'm worried. My security organisation has turned up an incident in her husband's youth that involved the death of a woman. It may merely be an uncomfortable coincidence, but I don't dare make that assumption.'

Meeting his hard eyes squarely, she said, 'I think you're right.'

His black brows lifted and his gaze sharpened. 'Just like that?' he said calmly, but his gaze didn't waver and Fleur had the uncomfortable feeling she was being skewered by a mind she knew to be extremely clever.

Trying to banish the defensive note in her words, she said, 'It happened to a friend of mine.'

He went still. 'Tell me about it.'

'He was her high-school boyfriend,' she said, looking away. 'He was always inclined to be jealous—Kim thought it meant he loved her. Well, so did I. But when he realised she wasn't going to marry him straight out of school, that she was going to university first, he just lost it.'

'How?' Luke frowned.

'He harassed her all through the Christmas holidays. He rang her incessantly, and he got drunk and said it was her fault, that she didn't love him because she was going away. He said they could get married and live in the sharemilker's cottage on his parents' farm. He'd always wanted to be a farmer, so he couldn't see why she wanted to go to university.'

'What happened?' Luke asked.

'In the end, her parents sent her away to stay with an aunt and uncle in Australia. She wrote to him from there, saying she thought it was better if they didn't see each other for a while. He didn't seem to care.He didn't try to contact Kim again, and it was a busy time on farms, what with haymaking and summer crops, so no one really noticed that he was a bit quiet.'

'Go on,' Luke said evenly.

'After the semester began he rang her up and asked her out, and she said no. She'd had time to think about what she really wanted, and it was to go to university. So he—he came down to the university hostel and talked her into going out with him for a drive in his car.' She stopped, staring into her coffee cup. Eventually she said quietly, 'I wasn't there, but even if I had been I wouldn't have—I would never have suspected anything. Deke drove her to a beach and then he shot her. And himself. He left a note, saying he couldn't face life without her so it was best they go together into the next life.'

She stopped, overcome by the memories.

Luke's warm hand enclosed hers, and he pulled her up and held her closely, offering the unspoken comfort of his strong body.

She said raggedly, 'None of us believed that Deke would ever harm Kim, not even when he was harassing her. He never threatened her—he gave no sign that he'd harm her. I'm glad you're looking out for your friend. Her husband might not be like poor Deke—she might be overreacting—but that's better than not taking any notice of the situation.'

Luke said something beneath his breath, then said in a goaded voice, 'I hope you didn't understand that.' Before she could answer he said, 'I'm sorry— I had no idea that telling you this would bring back memories of such a tragedy.'

'Of course you didn't.' She pulled herself away and he let her go. 'I still get a bit emotional thinking about Kim and the waste of their lives, but I'm over it.'

Luke said, 'I can hear the chopper. We have to go.'

'Why aren't we driving?'

He shrugged. 'The helicopter is faster.'

And safer, she thought as they flew over the sleeping island—no chance of anyone ambushing them on the narrow roads. Her stomach knotted.

Irrationally, she wanted to stay, to do what she could to protect Luke.

How stupid and futile was that!

But as they arrived at the plane, a sleek corporate jet, she said urgently, 'Won't you let me stay and be a decoy? I'm sure if Janna's husband realised that I'm the person—'

'No,' he said implacably.

She opened her mouth to object, and he covered it with his palm. 'No. It's simply not an option. Don't even think of it.'

Inside the plane, he said, 'You weren't responsible for your friend Kim's tragedy. Nothing you could have done would have prevented it.'

'I know that,' she said too quickly.

'Intellectually, yes, of course you do.' His gaze was darkly penetrating. 'But when you were telling me about it, you sounded as though you still feel that you should have noticed something that would have prevented their deaths. It's called survivor guilt, and it's useless.'

'I know,' she said miserably.

'Do exactly what my security man tells you to do, and don't go out of the apartment until you hear from me.'

She nodded, watching him walk out of the door and down the steps. A steward came up to her and said, 'This way, Miss Lyttelton.'

Numbly, because she knew she'd never see Luke again, she followed him to a seat, let him tuck her in and show her how the seat belt worked, refused anything to eat or drink, and listened to the note of the engines change pitch as the plane prepared to leave Fala'isi. The seat was superbly comfortable, the fittings luxurious yet she saw and felt nothing of them. Instead, she spent the hours travelling back to New Zealand worrying about what lay in wait for the man she loved in the tropical paradise he called home.

Luke rang the penthouse three days later. He sounded bleak, but when she asked him what had happened he brushed it off. 'He's dead,' he said briefly. 'And he didn't manage to kill Janna, which was what he intended. But she's a mess—emotionally,' he added hastily when Fleur gasped. 'No, he didn't hurt her. And his death was an accident, which makes things easier for everyone.'

'How—how did he die?'

'He drowned during a swim,' he said unemotionally. 'We had boats out looking for him, but his body was washed up this morning.'

'I see,' she said. What now? she wanted to ask. What will happen now?

Of course she knew. She'd go.

He said, 'I can't get back to Auckland immediately. Stay in the penthouse until I contact you again.'

Fleur wanted to know much more, but could tell that it would be useless asking. And she didn't need to answer such a direct order. 'I hope everything works out well for you.'

'I hope so, too,' he said curtly. 'I have to go. Take care, Fleur.'

'You, too.' It was all she could allow herself to say. Aching tears burned in her throat and at the back of her eyes as she replaced the receiver.

So she set her jaw and started making plans. The man who'd shared the penthouse with her during those interminable three days was her first hurdle.

To him she said casually, 'Have you heard from Mr Chapman?'

'Yes, I have. I'm to put myself at your disposal.'

She smiled. 'Which means that now any danger's past, you can go home. You won't miss your daughter's birthday tomorrow after all. If you give me a contact number I can ring you if I need anything.'

He thought about that, eventually saying, 'I wasn't given explicit clearance to leave you, but I can't see why I shouldn't take Anita to the zoo. She's been looking forward to it for weeks now.'

Feeling guilty, she said, 'Great.'

Back in her own bedroom, she looked at the wardrobe of clothes, paid for by Luke, that had somehow accompanied her to Auckland. Silk underwear and designer clothes had no place in her real life. But, however much her pride rebelled at taking any of them, she needed something to wear until she could earn the money to get sensible ones.

She packed the barest necessities into the smallest bag that had accompanied her to Auckland.

That done, she went out into the sitting room and looked around. Like Luke's house on Fala'isi it was superbly decorated, although in a much more urban style. And like that house it was a prison—possibly the most luxurious prison in the world, but it had driven her mad to languish here not knowing what was going on in Fala'isi.

She wondered what he was doing now. Looking after Janna, she thought, and wondered if her suspicions were correct. Had he decided to accept her as a guest so that Janna's husband would be put off? Had all this been a charade to protect a woman—possibly the woman he still loved?

Worse still, when he'd made love to her, had it all been for Janna?

Nauseated, she picked up the newspaper, and there, in the world section, she found an item of news. Heartbeats chasing each other, she gazed at the woman who'd come to haunt her life. The photograph was black and white, but she could see the resemblance, and if that mane of hair was the same colour as hers few people would be able to tell the difference at a distance.

She blinked fiercely, staunching swift, angry

tears, and forced herself to read the item. Apparently her husband, very wealthy and prominent in European circles, had suffered an accident while on holiday. His wife was shattered, and staying with friends until the inquest was finalised.

'Just one friend,' she said bleakly, giving the item a last look before she folded the paper and put it down.

In a way it was an affirmation of something she'd suspected ever since she'd found out that she looked like Janna. She'd noticed something different about Luke when he'd spoken of the other woman. Admittedly, it could just have been that she had contacted him again and he was wondering whether or not to believe her tales of abuse and fear, but it could also have been that he had never given up on her.

Fleur got up and walked into the bedroom she'd been given, one with an outlook down into the hotel courtyard. She ignored the manicured gardens and stared at herself in the mirror. Even if he didn't love Janna, that didn't mean he loved Fleur, she thought painfully.

After all, what had she to offer him? OK, so she'd coped with his social life, but if he hadn't been there to unobtrusively support her every inch of the way she'd have floundered and made an utter fool of herself.

And of him.

She thought of his parents, tall, aristocratic, good-looking, and wondered what they'd think of her. Certainly they wouldn't view her as any sort of match in a love affair, let alone a marriage.

She winced. That magic word—so far out of her reach that she should give up on it right now. The item in the newspaper reinforced her decision to leave so strongly she felt a surge of energy, as though instinct was warning her to go now.

By late afternoon the next day she was settling into a place that called itself a motel, though it catered to long-term residents rather than casual motorists, who'd usually opt for more salubrious surroundings.

At least she had her bankbook with her; it had been useless in Fala'isi, but now she was able to draw out enough money to keep herself going. And, as a precaution, she took out the very small amount left in the original account and used it to start another one in a different bank and under another name.

She had no idea whether Luke would look for her, but she suspected he would. That inherent protectiveness, she thought, and cringed at the idea of accepting more charity from him.

No, pride might be a cold bedfellow but it was better than the thorns of humiliation. She'd written Luke a letter exonerating the bodyguard, and thanking him in the most formal terms for his hospitality and his help. She was fine, she assured him, and she wished him all the best for his future life.

And, bearing in mind his statement that it was almost impossible for anyone to disappear if the searcher had money, she'd done everything she could think of to prevent him finding her.

'FLEUR, we need to talk.'

Fleur jumped at the sound of her employer's voice behind her. Without turning, she nodded. 'Yes, I suppose we do.'

'OK, leave that for a moment and come into the staffroom.'

Fleur put down the bag of potting mix she'd been transferring to the stand, and turned. Too quickly; her head buzzed, and she had to close her eyes to stop the world swinging wildly out of control around her.

In the cluttered staffroom the middle-aged woman who'd hired her to pot up seedlings and help in the roadside nursery filled the kettle. 'I'm assuming you can still drink tea,' she said dryly.

'I'm fine,' Fleur protested.

'You're as white as a ghost.' Efficiently Kath went about making tea, then pushed a mug across to her employee. 'When's the baby due?'

Fleur started, spilling the tea. Scrubbing away at the wet table with a tissue, she admitted, 'I—in about seven months.'

'I'm not happy seeing you lift heavy weights around.'

Fleur braced herself, but Kath continued, 'You'd better concentrate on light stuff from now on. Have you thought at all what you're going to do once the baby arrives?'

Fleur lifted her gaze and gave the ghost of a smile. 'Until yesterday I'd been refusing to accept that I'm pregnant.'

'I know the feeling,' her interrogator said wryly. 'However, hiding your head in the sand isn't going to help you. Have you told the father?'

Fleur shook her head. 'No.'

'Why?'

'Because he wouldn't be interested,' Fleur said, and knew as she said it that she was lying.

Of course Luke might not believe that the baby was his; he'd used protection. But, being Luke, he'd insist on DNA testing.

'I suspect he might be,' her employer said. She paused, then said, 'Tricia. Why Tricia?'

Fleur blinked, then realised that Kath had used her real name before, instead of the alias she'd been using since she'd fled Auckland for this provincial town in the heart of the North Island. Panic hollowed out her stomach.

Fighting it, she said, 'My mother's name. How did you know?'

The older woman held out a women's magazine. In it was a photograph—one taken at the charity function on Fala'isi. She was laughing; she remembered that Luke had said something funny and she'd thought she had never been so happy. It seemed so long ago, to have happened in another world to a different woman.

Her shocked gaze moved to the caption: *DO YOU KNOW THIS WOMAN?* it shouted.

And, underneath it, the word *REWARD* was even more prominently displayed.

Fleur gabbled, 'It isn't me—I know of her. She's some sort of actress, isn't she? I'm flattered that you think I look like her, but it's—'

'My dear, I think you need to accept that someone is looking for you.'

'But it's not me,' Fleur said desperately.

Kath just looked at her with shrewd eyes, and after a moment Fleur sagged. 'OK, so it is me,' she muttered.

The older woman said briskly, 'Is this someone who wants to find you likely to be your baby's father?'

'I—I suppose so,' Fleur admitted, because who else could it be?

'Are you afraid of him?' Kath probed, watching her with keen eyes.

Fleur's astonished exclamation ended on a cracked note. 'Of course I'm not!'

Apparently satisfied with her answers, the owner said, 'Why haven't you told him about the child?'

'I told you, he won't be interested.'

'Drink your tea. And while you're doing it, think very seriously about the ethics of not telling a man that you're carrying his child. It might seem to be the best thing you can do for the baby now, but how are you going to feel when she's twelve, and you can't afford the things she needs for high school? Or when he's fourteen and getting into trouble because you're working long hours and he has no father to be an example?'

Each word hit Fleur like a spear. Even while she'd been resisting the very idea of pregnancy, similar concerns and fears had plagued her. Avoiding any direct reply, she asked, 'Are you going to answer this?'

'No,' her employer said calmly, 'but sooner or later someone else will make the connection. It's inevitable, Fleur—and that name suits you much better than Tricia ever did, by the way!'

Fleur put her hands to her face and drew in a long, shuddering breath. 'I can't do it,' she said in a muted tone.

'You can. If he's not violent, why would you not?' When Fleur didn't answer Kath persisted, 'He was there when the baby was conceived—it's his responsibility as well as yours. And clearly he wants to find you.'

A fugitive colour burned her skin. 'That's the sort of man he is—responsible.'

'Then what do you have to lose?'

Pride.

Fleur looked down at her hands, resting loosely on the table. She could look after the baby—fashion some sort of life for it. But eventually her child would want to know why it didn't have a father.

Would it think—as she had when her father had left—that somehow the situation was its fault? She remembered how that had gnawed at her, staining her own childhood, and how she'd worried about her mother, working long hours to put food on the table.

She said wearily, 'All right—I'll contact him.'

Kath pushed the magazine in front of her. 'Do it now. Ring that 0800 number.'

Luke probably realised, Fleur thought with a pang of humiliation, that she simply didn't have the money to make a toll call.

'I'll do it tomorrow,' she said, getting to her feet.

Kath looked at her. 'Do it now, Fleur. Trust me, putting it off and running away again isn't sensible. If you don't ring that number now, I will.'

Fleur drew in a deep breath and said with a pale smile, 'You're a determined woman. You remind me very much of the baby's father.'

The baby, she thought, knowing that beneath her heart lay Luke's child. She picked up the portable phone, set her jaw and dialled the number.

The call was answered by a woman with a

pleasant voice. Fleur swallowed, then said thinly, 'My name is Fleur Lyttelton—'

'Hold the line, please,' the woman said crisply, and the next moment Fleur went white and swayed as she heard Luke's voice, tense and angry. 'Fleur, where the *hell* are you?'

She told him, and he said, 'Is anyone with you?'

'Yes.'

'Put whoever it is on, please.'

Rebuffed, she silently held out the receiver. Her face a study in lively astonishment, Kath took it and said, 'Hello.'

Fleur watched her face change expression to one of comprehension, and then to amazement as she said, 'Her employer. Yes, she's all right.' After something more from Luke, Kath said firmly, 'She won't do that. I'm quite sure of it.' And she gave him the address of the nursery.

Then she put the telephone down and looked at Fleur with shock and interest. 'Luke Chapman? The Pacific Island Chapman family?'

'Yes,' Fleur said numbly.

'Hmm. Very well, he'll be here within a couple of hours, so wherever he is it's reasonably close. I'm to make sure you don't run.'

'Of course I won't run.'

But when the car drew up outside she flinched, and her employer said urgently, 'Tell me now—has he ever hurt you? I don't just mean physically but—emotionally?'

'I swear to you on my mother's memory that he hasn't,' Fleur said with such quiet confidence that it rang totally true. 'It's just that…I love him and he doesn't love me.'

The older woman's eyes were kind and wise. 'Don't give up.' She watched a tall figure get out of the car and stride towards the shop. 'You're a damned nice person, and you've got something he wants. You can build on that.'

Sensible words, but in her heart of hearts Fleur knew that second best was almost worse than nothing at all. What she wanted from Luke was just too far out of her reach.

She braced herself, met a pair of condemning ice-grey eyes, and gulped.

If only she could collapse now! But, no. Her body might feel boneless, but her eyes were greedily devouring every contour of his beloved face and a tide of awareness, of eager anticipation, surged through her.

For the first time since he'd left her on the jet on Fala'isi she felt alive again.

He said between his teeth, 'What the hell have you been doing to yourself? You look like death!'

Her employer made a swift movement, and he turned on her. 'What's she been doing?' he demanded.

'Working and fretting,' Kath said succinctly.

Fleur interrupted. 'I'm fine,' she said. And stopped, not knowing how to carry on when her employer was bristling like a guard dog at her side and Luke was about to hear something that would shock and dismay him.

Luke smiled, and with resignation Fleur watched Kath succumb to that blazing charm without even a pretence at resistance.

'Thank you for taking her in when she ran away,' he said calmly. 'I'm afraid she won't be coming back to work, but if I can help with getting you a new hand I'll be happy to do so.'

'That's very thoughtful of you,' Kath said, clearly reassured, 'but I have emergency help I can call on until I get someone else. Take care of her.'

'I will,' he said decisively.

Ten minutes later Fleur was ensconced in the back of the hire car, and an hour later, all arrangements made, she was sitting once more in the jet as they flew towards Auckland.

CHAPTER ELEVEN

FLEUR's eyelids drifted slowly down. The muffled noise of the jet engines acted like a lullaby, and as Luke had gone to confer with the pilots she was no longer kept in a state of simmering awareness.

She was so tired. Sheer willpower had kept her going these past couple of months, but now that Luke had taken over she no longer needed to be alert and active.

Weak, she thought, drowsily wondering how on earth she'd stayed strong for the years of her mother's illness only to succumb to this humiliating dependence.

She woke to the sound of Luke's voice. 'Wake up,' he insisted, an arm slipping around her shoulder. 'We're almost there. Once we land you can sleep as long as you like.'

Reluctantly she forced heavy lashes up and met his eyes, cool and commanding. He looked older, she thought in confusion, and somehow even more formidable. The aura of anger she'd felt before was gone, replaced by an intimidating, controlled authority.

'I'm sorry,' she blurted.

His brows lifted. 'For running away? I should damned well hope so—but we can talk about that later. Do you want to wash your face?'

Colour stormed through her skin as she realised she was nestled against him, one hand clutching his shirt. Jerking away, she said, 'Yes, thank you.'

'Then you'd better hurry up.' He looked satisfied, as though somehow he'd proved something to himself.

Probably that she couldn't keep her hands off him, she thought bleakly.

He drove her to the penthouse. She stayed silent when they went up in the lift, but once inside she said bluntly, 'What happens now?'

'We talk about unfinished business.' He sent her a swift, mocking glance. 'You may have forgotten what happened just before we parted, but I haven't.'

Fleur fought back the instinct to curve a protective hand over the place where his child nestled within her. Why on earth had she let him abduct her like this? She must have been mad!

Too late to object now, though. However, she'd show him she wasn't a pushover.

'Oh, your reputation as a superb lover is intact,' she said, shocking herself with the cool insolence of her tone. 'Of course I hadn't forgotten.'

'Just as well,' he drawled in a voice made dangerous by the thread of icy anger running through the words. He flung his next words like a challenge. 'Perhaps the question you have to ask—and answer—is why you let yourself be brought here.'

Stung, she hurled back, 'Because I have to tell you that I'm pregnant, and I—' Appalled at her stupidity, she searched his handsome face, green eyes widening as she saw it harden.

She took a sharp, shallow breath and finished defiantly, 'We need to talk about that, but before we start there's one thing that's not negotiable. I'm not going to have an abortion.'

His face darkened. 'Dead right,' he ground out. 'At least we're agreed on that.' Without hesitation he went on, 'You're pale again—I'll bring you something to drink and then you can rest.'

'I don't need to rest.' And she wouldn't be able to until they'd discussed this. She added with a humourless grimace, 'No coffee, please.'

He surveyed her face with merciless intensity. 'We'll work something out, Fleur. Just take things as they come, all right?'

In her bedroom she found the clothes she'd left behind in the wardrobe. Apparently Luke had been certain he'd find her.

A shiver ran through her. No, been utterly determined to find her, she thought. But why, when he didn't know about the baby?

That blasted sense of responsibility again. He'd look after her because he felt he should. And he'd probably make sure his child was cared for and educated while having as little contact with its mother as he could manage.

Well, that would be better for all of them.

She showered and came out into the room in her wrap, to find a tray of tea on the table in the window. Resigning herself to the inevitable, she dressed in a pair of ivory trousers and a loose silk top, slipped her feet into sandals and allowed herself a bittersweet, nostalgic thought for Fala'isi. She'd probably never see it again...

She'd just finished the tea when someone knocked on the door. Luke, of course. After another penetrating survey he said, 'You look more like yourself. Can I come in?'

'Yes, of course.'

He said abruptly, 'There's no *of course* about it. You can tell me to leave you alone if you want to.'

'No.' Better get this over and done with.

But when they were seated in the armchairs in the window he seemed content to examine her with a frowning gaze.

Finally, when her nerves were so on edge she

jumped a little, he asked curtly, 'Why did you run away?'

It now seemed a stupid thing to have done—over-dramatic and foolish. She said, 'I didn't need to stay. Once Janna's husband died I wasn't in any danger, if I ever had been.'

'You had been,' he said with grim authority. 'He'd planned to ambush us on the road and kill us both. He had a long-range rifle in his possession, with telescopic sights and night vision.'

She shivered. 'Did he...was there a confrontation?' she asked in a subdued voice, her green eyes smoky with some indecipherable emotion.

Reining in the seething emotions that had been building ever since she'd run away, Luke said more moderately, 'Yes.'

All colour fled from her skin and her hands clenched in her lap. 'What happened?' she asked in a ghost of a voice.

When he hesitated she burst out with swift passion, 'I want to know, Luke! I'm not some fragile flower that has to be protected from cold winds.'

Yes, she could cope. 'I had him picked up—without the rifle—and brought to the house. He refused to believe you weren't Janna until I showed him the shots from the charity function.'

Even then, the man had insisted they must have been tampered with, firmly in the grip of his obsession. It had taken Luke several hours to convince him that he was on a wild-goose chase. 'In the end, he accepted that not only was Janna not on the island, but that you were the woman who'd been with me.'

Then Fleur asked the question he'd been expecting. 'How did he drown?'

'I put a guard on him until he could get on a plane out of Fala'isi, and sent him out to the house on the island—the one we went to the day Sue Baxter got into difficulties.'

Eyes enormous, she nodded.

Luke went on, 'It's too far from the shore of the main island to swim. He told his guard he wanted to snorkel. It seemed a reasonable request, so he was allowed it. He tried to make it across the lagoon but drowned before his guard could reach him.'

He might have been talking about an incident on the road for all the emotion she could discern in his tone. 'And Janna?'

'She's grieving.' He shrugged, his handsome face stern. 'I think at first she did love him, until he abused her. She certainly had reason to fear him.'

'Is she still on the island?' Too late, Fleur desperately wanted to call the words back. They made her sound pathetic and needy.

'She came back for the inquest, but she's in London now.'

Fleur wondered again whether he still loved the woman he'd done so much to protect.

Still in that same steady voice he asked, 'When did you realise you were pregnant?'

She bit her lip. 'The day before yesterday. Until then I wondered whether there was something else wrong—whether I'd caught some tropical disease—because I was tired all the time.'

He said something beneath his breath and she lifted her head. 'I never thought of pregnancy because you used protection.' Painful colour stung her skin. 'And I've never been regular. But I finally accepted it might be a baby, so I bought a test and it was positive.'

Even then she might have gone on hiding her head in the sand if Kath hadn't taxed her with it.

She waited for him to ask her whether the child was his, but he said merely, 'I'll lodge a Notice of Intended Marriage with the registrar here, which means we can be married in three days' time.'

Fleur stared at him, her eyes enormous in her pale face. She literally couldn't think of what to say as violent and opposed emotions warred for supremacy—huge, mindless elation and relief, and total fury that he'd do this without consulting her. And a soul-deep grief, because she loved him so much and she was going to refuse him.

'How do you know that?' she demanded.

He leaned back in his chair and watched her, his attitude one of complete control, his handsome, arrogant face inscrutable. 'I rang from the plane to find out. Marriage is the inevitable next step.'

Grittily she said, 'I believe the usual thing is to ask. My answer is no.'

One black brow lifted in cool question. 'So why did you contact me?'

'Not to…to demand marriage,' she spluttered. 'Because I thought you should know.'

Luke's eyes narrowed, his mouth compressing into a cynical smile. 'Believe me, if you hadn't told me I'd have been very angry. And I intend to support my child, so it seems to me that the best thing we can do is marry.'

She said harshly, 'That's not necessary. I won't deny you access if you want it.'

'We were good together,' he said casually, that hint of French accent colouring his deep voice. 'I'll do my best to make you happy.'

'What about you?'

He shrugged, his expression cynically amused. 'I won't find being married to you any hardship.'

Hardship? Fury surged through her, and a deep, bitter desolation. 'Do you realise how insulting that is?' she demanded.

'I didn't plan for a baby, nor to get married, but I'm not going to turn my back on either you or the child, paying out and just visiting occasionally,' he said with silky distinctness, watching her with a hooded, dangerous gaze. 'I grew up in a family that holds its relationships dear. This will be my parents' first grandchild. But, apart from that, I don't want a son or daughter who doesn't know me. As for insulting—what is insulting about being told that I find you desirable and interesting and that I look forward to having you for my wife?'

Hot tears blurred his face as she said raggedly, 'It would be a recipe for disaster. My parents loved each other when they married—my mother loved my father until she died!—but that didn't stop the marriage from disintegrating when he found someone he loved more. What sort of chance would we have?'

'A much better one than theirs,' he said tersely.

'Why?'

'Because we know exactly what we're doing, and why. Think, Fleur! I can offer you fidelity and support and in turn I ask the same. This is the only way to give our child the kind of loving home and family I grew up in, and that your father should have provided for you.'

'He fell in love with someone else,' she said numbly, so torn by longing it physically hurt.

Luke's contemptuous face told her what he felt. 'He already had a lover, a responsibility,' he said coldly. 'What sort of man was he to turn his back on you?'

She said with quiet desperation, 'Luke, I don't think this is a good idea. I don't want to be only a responsibility.' And, in a final attempt, she cried, 'You're sounding just like Gabrielle when she told me what sort of marriage she planned with you.'

He cut her short by getting to his feet in one lithe movement and pulling her to hers. Looking down at her face, he said with an ironic smile, 'Clearly I'm doing this all wrong, probably because I've never proposed to anyone before. You may object, but neither of us can alter the fact that I'm responsible for this situation and for the child you carry—my child. But of course you're both infinitely more to me than just a responsibility!'

She wanted so much to give in, to surrender to the desire that heated her blood and coiled through her like a particularly seductive snake, promising her untold pleasure, the answer to all the barely formed dreams that had tormented her these past months.

He said, 'Incidentally, Gabrielle is now very much in love with my cousin Vao. They're enjoying a very restrained, very chaste affair that just might end in marriage.'

Vao was the film star she'd met at the charity dinner. Fleur gave a bleak little smile, but said quietly, 'I'm glad of that. But I won't let you persuade me into this. I need time to think.'

'Perhaps you need something else,' he said, his gaze on her mouth.

Fleur whispered, 'No,' but surrendered anyway, returning the kiss with her heart in her sigh, in her yielding body.

When it was over he said against her lips, 'Perhaps a compromise.'

She stiffened in his arms, pulling away.

He let her go, but kept his eyes on her face. 'We'll marry, because our child deserves to know that its parents thought enough of it to make such a commitment. And we'll live together. But we'll take things very slowly. In time you might come to believe that I will be a good husband and father.'

'It's too risky,' she said unevenly. 'You're crowding me, and I can't think straight.'

'What is there to think of?' he demanded, a touch of arrogant impatience in his tone. 'You have only two choices. Either you marry me, or you do not.'

'And if I don't—what then?'

His expression settled into one she was beginning to recognise—an implacable determination. 'You will have to face the fact that I will sue for custody of the child.'

Fleur said harshly, 'You'll never get custody—not here in New Zealand.'

'Perhaps not,' he agreed, 'and it would be hugely

unpleasant for both of us and for the child.' He took her hand and drew her towards him.

'Fleur, there's no need for this,' he said, his voice deep and calm and utterly sure. 'I understand how you feel—believe me, I don't offer marriage lightly! And we've gone about this all wrong. But now we must work with the situation we have made together. Would it be so hard to be married to me? You enjoyed Fala'isi, didn't you?'

'You know I did,' she admitted reluctantly, aware that she was weakening.

'And you enjoyed the conception of our child,' he murmured, his voice flicking every nerve in her body into instant awareness.

Her skin burned and her mouth dried. She couldn't speak and he smiled, and dropped a kiss on her forehead and said, 'So did I.'

'I won't let you manipulate me with sex,' she muttered.

'It seems to be the only way I *can* manipulate you,' he said on a half-laugh. 'But I'm trying to be frank. If you don't want to make love again until you fully trust me, that's fine. But I want to make this child feel that he or she belongs, that there will always be a family to back him or her up. Don't you want that?'

Did he know how those few words stripped away her reservations?

Probably, she thought achingly, but, oh, how could she deny her child that comfort—the knowledge that whatever happened in its life there would always be family for it?

Tensely, her hands gripped so tightly together she could feel them starting to hurt, she said, 'Of course I do.'

'So, it is decided,' he said. If he'd shown even the slightest triumph she might have balked, but he didn't; his steel-grey eyes were warm when he picked up her tense hands and kissed one palm and then the other. 'You're exhausted, and the days ahead are going to be very busy. Go to bed now.'

Hours later, when she was lying in the bed by herself listening to the sounds of a city settling down for the night, Fleur had never felt so lonely in all her life.

She should have refused, she thought, panicking, but he'd known exactly how to appeal to her—the offer of a family for the baby, of support, of fidelity...

But what if his family hated her? And what if he'd lied? Or if their marriage made him unhappy...?

The next three days were a whirlwind of preparations. She was thoroughly checked over by a doctor, a pleasant middle-aged woman who specialised in prenatal care, and who pronounced her fit and perfectly normal.

Quaking, she met his parents when they flew in from Fala'isi—his tall, handsomely severe father, who examined her with guarded detachment, and his lovely mother with eyes a softer shade of grey than her son and a smile that welcomed her in while reserving judgement.

They didn't hate her, but naturally they were concerned. However, they attended the small wedding held in the exquisite seaside garden of a friend of Luke's. So did his sisters, Louise and Persis, both of whom had inherited their parents' stature, so that Fleur felt like a midget amongst them. She wore silk chiffon the colour of old ivory, with the exquisite pearl pendant Luke had lent her on Fala'isi, and carried a small posy over a prayer book.

They ate a delicious lunch at the friend's house. There were toasts, and much laughter, and many kisses when at last she and Luke left.

'All right?' he asked as the car drew away from the magnificent cliff-top home.

Fleur hid an incipient yawn with her hand. 'Thank you,' she said quietly. 'It was a lovely wedding.'

'Thank my mother,' he said with a smile. 'She pulled it together. You look—superb. Every man there envied me.'

Colour skimmed her cheekbones. She'd expected to be terrified and awkward and out of place, but she thought she'd held her end up reasonably well.

Thanks to Persis, who'd noticed her nerves before the wedding and said bracingly, 'Look, we're like the rest of human-ity—we're silly and sensible and stupid and clever and ordinary and absolutely bloody miraculous in turn! But we're all ordinary people.' She'd given her a sly, sideways glance and said, 'Even Luke, for all you gaze at him as though he's a god—which is very bad for him because he's high-handed enough without that!'

They spent the week of their honeymoon in a lodge high in the Southern Alps that overlooked the cold blue expanse of an alpine lake and a jagged line of pristine white peaks beyond. Belonging to the Chapman family, it was ultra-luxurious and exquisite. They had separate bedrooms, and although Fleur told herself to be grateful she longed for the comfort of Luke's arms.

Apart from that gnawing hunger for him, he was the perfect companion—considerate, amusing, interesting. In fact, everything that a woman could want, she thought dismally.

And after that interlude they flew to Fala'isi in the private jet.

CHAPTER TWELVE

LUKE drove them home. When they passed the entrance to his parents' house he said, 'My mother suggested we have dinner with them tomorrow night. They want to introduce you to a few of the locals. I agreed.'

Fleur sat tensely beside him, an odd sense of homecoming battling with a bleak foreboding that she had just made the biggest mistake of her life. She said stiffly, 'Yes, all right.'

He sent her a cool sideways glance. 'You might as well get it over with sooner than later.'

'I like your parents, and I know I'll enjoy dinner with them, but it would have been nice to have been asked rather than told.'

'I asked you to stay at the penthouse until I got there, but clearly you don't respond to requests.'

'You *ordered* me to stay,' she said, just as coldly. 'Once I wasn't in danger any more I left. I hope you didn't punish the security man.'

A tiny muscle flicked in the angle of his jaw. 'No. And leave it for now,' he said, taking the road over the mountain spur a fraction too fast.

'I hope,' she said, because it had to be faced, 'that you won't make any more arrangements without consulting me. I'm not used to it.'

After a fraught few seconds he sent her an amused smile that was tinged with apology. 'I know, and no, I won't turn into a domestic tyrant. My mother rang last night after you'd gone to bed, and I forgot about it until now.'

She returned his smile with a more restrained one, thinking despairingly that it took so little to stir her aching hunger into life: the tone of his beautiful voice when he said her name, the lift of one eyebrow, the fascinating way his mouth tucked into a smile...

Every day she was falling deeper and deeper into this consuming, dangerous enchantment. It scared her. Instead of weakly surrendering she should be searching for a way out of the snare of his masculinity before she lost herself, as her mother had done, unable to free herself from depending on one man for everything in life.

They drew up outside the house, its shutters wide open and the sun dazzling on the flowers in the sprawling gardens.

'Home,' Luke said.

That one word revealed the intensity and depth of

his feelings for this place. Fleur wondered forlornly if one day he might say her name that way, as though it was all he ever wanted on this earth.

And told herself not to be so stupid. He'd been brutally frank about his reasons for their marriage, not mentioning the word *love* once. Longing for something she could never have was a waste of time and energy and emotions. She'd made her decision; she still thought it was the right one, and she simply had to get on with it.

They walked into their first crisis, one Luke realised with baffled anger that he should have foreseen. Normally in full control of his life, he hadn't given it a thought until a beaming Susi led them into the main bedroom—flowers everywhere, the potent witchery of frangipani, sweet-scented candles flickering against the dusk.

A room prepared for lovers, not for two people who hadn't shared a bed in marriage.

Fleur froze, and he glanced down as colour rose in her silken skin. *My wife,* he thought, startled at the fierce possessiveness that gripped him.

He was about to make some comment when she said to Susi, 'Oh—this is so lovely! How kind you are! Thank you all so much.'

Her smile was tremulous. He saw tears gather in her eyes and slipped his arm around her shoulders, adding his thanks, teasing a flushing Susi until she said with a great laugh, 'Did you think we'd let your marriage pass without notice? You just wait until you see what the chef's prepared, although he's been threatening to storm out because you didn't give him a time for dinner.'

'In half an hour,' Luke told the housekeeper, who left, still chuckling.

Fleur moved out from under his shoulder. 'What do we do now?' she said in a subdued voice.

She pretended to examine the room—huge, more of a suite than a bedroom, with a sofa and chairs and a desk, just in case he felt the need to do some work in the middle of the night, no doubt. Even so, it was dominated by the bed.

'Don't worry. As you can see, there's plenty of sleeping area. You'll take the bed.' His voice was level, without emotion. 'I'll sleep on the sofa. And as soon as the baby becomes obvious you can say you'd prefer to sleep on your own.'

Fleur checked out the massive tester with posts draped in white mosquito netting. 'You'll be too uncomfortable on the sofa,' she said, terrified at the thought of spending nights in the same room.

She glanced at him, and then away again, and her heart cramped. He wore the formidable expression that meant he was going to get his own way. 'Can't we say that I'm used to sleeping on my own?'

'Only if you want the news that our marriage is

on the rocks to reach New Zealand in half an hour and England before morning.' He sounded aloof, as though the subject bored him.

'Would that be so bad?'

He shrugged. 'If you don't mind.'

Maybe she was making too much of this; too many protests might mean he'd realise that she was eating her heart out for him. And once he knew that she'd be an embarrassment to him—the wife who loved him when he couldn't return it—he'd treat her with exquisite courtesy, and a distance that would prevent her from clinging.

Pride lifted her head. 'Oh, what the hell! It seems horrid to spoil their pleasure when they've gone to so much trouble. But it makes far more sense if I sleep on the sofa—you're too big.'

He eyed her, his gaze cold and his mouth a thin, hard line. 'Just once,' he said with frigid politeness, 'it would be pleasant if you stopped objecting to everything and did as I suggest.'

'You don't suggest—you command!' she snapped back.

His mouth twitched. 'This is our second disagreement on that subject. You sound like my sisters.'

Fleur fought back an unwilling smile. 'They obviously know you well—why don't you listen to them occasionally? You won't be comfortable on the sofa, and I will.'

He said, 'Nevertheless you'll sleep in the bed. Now, we'd better get ready to eat whatever the chef's prepared.'

So, after forcing down a delicious meal and thanking its chief architect, she found herself walking towards that huge room. At the door Luke said formally, 'I have things to check in the office. I'll be back in half an hour or so.'

The bathroom was set up for someone of Luke's physique—a large shower, with the rose far enough up the wall that it wouldn't hit his head. Feeling like an intruder, she used it, then examined the clothes that had been lovingly unpacked into drawers in her own walk-in wardrobe.

Tamsyn Chapman had bought her a trousseau wardrobe, eagerly aided and abetted by her daughters. Fleur was touched and grateful for their kindness and their skill at choosing garments that shimmered on her, turning her into some radiant being she'd never seen before. Now, however, she looked at the semi-transparent gossamer garments in soft peaches and greens and pale translucent blues with mounting apprehension. Made to arouse and dazzle, they were shockingly inappropriate for the marriage she and Luke had entered into.

Hysterically she thought that a nice Mother Hubbard in some thick, unbreachable cotton would be more suitable.

Failing that, she chose the least revealing, a satin shirt with matching trousers, and made herself up a bed on the sofa, curling up on a couple of the pillows and beneath one of the cool linen sheets, wishing fervently that it was cold enough to hide herself in quilts and duvets and blankets.

A fur rug sounded like a brilliant idea, too.

Dead on the dot of half an hour the door opened and Luke came in. He stopped when he saw her there and his eyes narrowed. 'Get into the bed,' he said calmly.

She started to sit up, but sank back when the sheet slipped to reveal one almost bare shoulder. Cheeks coined with heat, she realised that the top button of her shirt had come undone, revealing too much of her shoulder and the curve of her breast. She ducked beneath the crisp embrace of the sheet and said, 'I'm perfectly all right here.'

In a quiet, ominous tone Luke said, 'I'm going to have a shower, and if you aren't in that bed when I come back I'll pick you up and put you there.'

'Oh, all right!' she snapped. 'If it's so important to you, then feel free to make yourself uncomfortable.'

His smile was sardonic. 'Believe me, I couldn't be any more uncomfortable than I am now!'

Fleur waited until he'd gone into the bathroom, then scuttled off the sofa and into the bed, slapping the book she'd been reading for the past three days onto the bedside table. It had been excellent reading, dull enough to send her to sleep every night, but now the print danced in front of her eyes and after several attempts to read a sentence she discarded it, switched off the bedside lamp and huddled under the sheet, closing her eyes and willing herself to relax.

Every muscle in her body remained obstinately tight. She drew in a deep breath and began to tense and then ease her muscles, starting from her toes and working upwards.

Although the house wasn't air-conditioned, the thick coral walls kept it cool. Not, however, if you were on high alert and torn by a turbulent mixture of erotic hunger and antagonism. By the time the click of the bathroom door announced Luke's return perspiration was starting to gather at Fleur's temples. She fought back the desire to open her eyes.

'I'm back,' he said, softly enough not to disturb her if she'd been asleep.

'OK,' she mumbled.

Tautly she waited, her straining ears picking up the barely discernible sounds of his progress to the sofa. He moved like a predator, she thought, a hot thrill working its way across her heated skin.

The unexpected sound of his voice made her jump.

'Goodnight, Fleur.'

'Goodnight,' she muttered.

Lying there in Luke's bed she counted sheep,

then, when her brain remained obdurately alert, sub-
stituted dolphins for them. Nothing happened. She
was turning over for about the tenth time when she
realised he'd hear her tossing about. After that she
lay rigidly still.

Eventually silence and darkness proclaimed that
it would be safe to open her tightly clamped eyes.
No light shone in the room, but rays from the moon
probed the shutters, sending a faint tracery of bars
across the floor. When her eyes became night-
attuned she could make out the furniture, and
Luke's shape on the big sofa. He had to be uncomfortable, she thought, and wondered why on earth
he was so insistent she take the bed.

But what did she know about men, and especially
a man like Luke? Born to command, raised to be responsible, highly intelligent, he was different from
any other man she'd known.

Eventually she slid into sleep on a feverish fantasy
of her and Luke in the big bed, making love, his
hands cupping her face as he kissed her, and then
skimming down to caress her breasts…

She woke to sunlight, and an overwhelming sense
of wellbeing. Fully dressed, Luke had just pushed the
shutters open so that the day poured in, soft and fresh
and filled with the music of the waves on the reef.

'Good morning,' he said formally, but his eyes
were amused as he came towards her.

Pretending to close her eyes against the light, she blocked him out, and the fragments of her dreams slid softly into the mists of the night.

Luke stopped beside the bed and looked down at her. 'How did you sleep?'

Her lashes came up and she fixed him with a wide, dazed gaze. 'Like a log, thank you.' Her voice was drowsy and soft, husky with promises she didn't even know she was making.

Every cell in Luke's body fired in response to her sleepy smile. Her smoky green eyes were half covered by long lashes, her hair gleaming fire on the pillow, mouth soft and sensuous. The contrast between her face—that of a siren—and the innocent, subtle sexiness of the satin pyjama top tightened his vocal cords so that his voice emerged harsh and abrupt.

'Your wrap's on the end of the bed,' he said. 'Breakfast will be ready on the terrace in half an hour.'

And he got out of there before he forgot his promise not to touch her. She was far too tempting for her own good.

Fleur yawned, then eased herself out of the bed to sit on its side. She sighed, thinking that she should be delighted that Luke had remained on the sofa. Instead she found herself suffering from a profound feeling of anticlimax.

She hoped she hadn't snored. Suppressing a

startled giggle, she went into the bathroom. It gave her an illicit pleasure to turn on the shower he'd just used.

How foolish was that!

Not much later, showered and dressed in a pair of slim cream linen pants, matching sandals and a soft floaty top in cream and the clear green of her eyes, she went out onto the terrace.

Although the table was set, Luke wasn't there. She looked up into the deep blue sky. Everything had changed, she thought confusedly. She was no longer the woman who'd come to Fala'isi to fulfil a promise to her mother. Loving Luke had fundamentally changed her.

'That's a big sigh,' Luke observed from behind, startling her with his noiseless arrival.

Whirling around, she met speculative grey eyes. He walked out into the sunlight, his expression cool and controlled.

'I was just thinking that this is a wonderful place,' she told him honestly.

'As close to paradise as you'll get in this world,' he said, using the island's catchphrase for tourism.

She nodded. 'Absolutely.'

A dove cooed from one of the big trees around the edge of the lawn. In spite of her tumultuous emotions, Fleur felt strangely at home, as though this place had always been waiting for her.

Luke smiled down at her, his momentary aloofness fading under the impact of his charm. Her heart picked up speed, and she returned his smile with a shy, involuntary one of her own. She loved him so much, yet he was a stranger to her—always would be, because he didn't love her. The dove cooed again, a seductive, tranquil sound on the rapidly warming air.

During breakfast she sensed a subtle withdrawal that hadn't been there the previous night, even when he'd been so angry with her in his bedroom. Probably now that he was home he was facing the fact that the baby had tied him with its innocent presence as effectively as it had chained her.

His voice broke into her thoughts. 'Does the smell of coffee affect you?'

'Not too much.'

But when he moved the coffeepot to the end of the table and poured himself a cup of tea, she said in a dismayed voice, 'You don't have to give it up.'

His brows lifted. 'I'm not going to make you uncomfortable just because I like coffee in the morning. Have you suffered any morning sickness?'

'No.' She grimaced. 'I just feel tired all the time. Apart from that, I'm fine. But I can't help wondering why something that's an entirely natural process should exhaust me so much.' She sipped fruit juice before saying enviously, 'Apparently other women bloom.'

'Some,' Luke agreed. 'Others wilt badly.'

She grinned, an elusive dimple playing beside her mouth for a second. 'Middle of the road,' she said in a resigned voice. 'Sounds like me.'

'I don't think there's much that's middle of the road about you.' Luke leaned back and subjected her to a merciless scrutiny that had her mentally squirming.

'You gave up your dreams to look after your mother. And, although you clearly didn't want to, you contacted me when you discovered you were pregnant because you realised you didn't have the resources to care for a child the way it deserves to be cared for. It seems that responsibility is engrained in your character.'

Startled, she stared at him, a tiny cautious hope lighting inside her. Perhaps they did have something in common, after all.

Then pragmatism took hold. They shared a baby and a sense of responsibility. Big deal. Not enough to build a satisfactory marriage on.

'I looked after my mother because I loved her, and because there was no one else,' she said. 'I couldn't leave her to care-givers.' Her fingers curved protectively at her waist before she realised what she was doing and dropped her hand self-consciously back into her lap. 'And the baby—I know what it's like to be alone. My father rejected me; I hoped you wouldn't do that to this one.'

'What would you have done if I had?'

Surprised, she returned, 'I never thought of it.'

A dark brow lifted. 'Why not?' he asked neutrally.

'I don't know.' Her forehead wrinkled and she looked across the lawn to where the sun highlighted a swathe of crimson creeper in a shaft of gold. Talking like this—revealing her innermost emotions—was dangerous, but if they were to forge any sort of relationship for the sake of their child she had to drop some of her defences.

'Because I already knew you felt strongly about your responsibilities, I suppose.' She stopped and asked, 'Why did you get your investigators to look for me?'

He shrugged. 'Several reasons. I wanted to make sure you weren't pregnant—yes, I know we used protection, but it's not infallible. And I felt that you'd got tangled up in something that wasn't your affair just because you happen to have the same colouring and general air of a woman I'd once known very well.'

'Responsibility again,' she said, adding ruefully, 'I think I'm seeing a theme here.'

'For both of us, it seems, it goes with the territory,' he said with an odd little smile. He glanced at his watch. 'And part of my responsibilities is a meeting with the local council of chiefs in an hour, so I'd better get going. What do you plan to do today?'

'I don't know. Is there anything you want me to do?'

'I think you should relax.'

She said, 'I can't do that all the time. I'd like to learn the local language, so our baby can be brought up speaking three languages, too.'

'I'll organise a teacher, but you'll learn it faster if you tell the staff and ask them to speak it to you.' He got to his feet. 'You've got that fine-drawn look of someone almost at the end of her resources. Take it easy. Sleep this afternoon. Do you want someone to do your hair for this dinner party tonight?'

A chill beneath her ribs spread. 'Do I need to?'

He subjected her to another of those penetrating inspections. 'Only if you want to.'

'I don't want to embarrass your parents,' she said anxiously.

Luke's frown took her by surprise. 'You won't,' he said shortly. 'It might help you to know that my mother came to the island as a perfectly ordinary New Zealand woman, secretary to a businessman. We're not snobs, Fleur.'

'I know that,' she defended herself sturdily. 'Your family is charming. I like them immensely. It's just that—well, family background is important to the islanders. Your family background in particular, for all sorts of social and symbolic reasons.'

'The islanders aren't snobs either,' he said. 'Yes, heritage is important, but it's not everything. Character counts for a lot. My mother is almost universally loved. Don't worry about what people think of you—it's not an issue, although learning to speak Fala'isian will please them immensely.'

He extended a hand, and when she took it drew her to her feet. Very quietly he said, 'You belong to me now; you're a Chapman. This is your home now.' A wry smile creased his tanned face. 'Believe me, there will be times when you'll find our close family ties are a damned nuisance, but they're inescapable. Get used to the idea.'

He leaned down and dropped a kiss on her forehead—the kind of kiss, she thought forlornly as she watched him go back inside the house, that he might have given a much younger cousin.

The day stretched out before her like an eternity. Even in paradise, she discovered, you needed something to do for time to have meaning. She spent some of it exploring the grounds, and some reading in the shade of the big tree. She swam, and after lunch she slept in Luke's huge, alien bedroom, first closing the wooden shutters that dimmed the light yet let in the cooling breeze.

She was woken by a sharp knock on the door. Groggy with sleep, she sat up and stared around. The knock was repeated; it came, she realised, not from the door that led to the rest of the house, but from outside.

Yawning, she pushed her hair back from her face and got to her feet, staggering slightly. She'd slept in the pyjamas she'd worn the previous night, so she snagged up her wrap and shrugged into it as she crossed towards the shutters and opened a shutter.

Outside stood a woman. Fleur gaped, her mind still hazy with sleep. 'What do you want?' she asked foolishly.

'To talk to you,' the woman said, pushing past her and into the room.

'Hey!' Her vision clearing, Fleur noticed the tumble of dark red hair down the woman's back. A surge of adrenalin boosted her into action. She said evenly, 'Janna, I presume?'

'And you are the nobody everyone says has just married Luke.' The words were said with a distinct snap. 'Is it true?'

'I don't know what business it is of yours, but, yes.' Fleur groped for some handle on reality, astounded that she should finally be face to face with the woman who'd, until then, been a shadowy figure in the background.

She was beautiful, with perfect features and a curvy body that proclaimed a lush sensuality, and she oozed confidence and sophistication. Fleur felt totally, humiliatingly inadequate.

Janna said curtly, 'I know he's not one to turn

down a willing female, but, damn it, how the hell did you get him to marry you?'

Flushing with anger, Fleur asked, 'What are you doing here?'

Janna's lush mouth tightened. 'I've spent far more time here than you have. I can see why Luke took you to bed—he wanted to marry me, you know. I'd have done it, too, only it meant living in this god-forsaken hole! When I turned him down and married Eric he was shattered.' She raked Fleur with a disparaging glance. 'I'd have expected him to choose someone a bit more up-market, but men aren't exactly noted for their finesse or their pickiness, are they? I suppose he saw that hair and decided you'd do until he could get me out of his system.'

Her words were like slime, smearing over Fleur's precarious happiness. Her hand stole to her waist. Stiffly, her tone expressing her distaste, she said, 'Go now, please.'

But Janna had noticed the betraying movement, and she dragged in a sharp, accusing breath. 'So you got pregnant, did you? Clever of you—he hides it well, but Luke's very dynastic. Take it from me, make sure you get as much as you can from him in cold hard cash before he divorces you. And there's one thing you should know—he killed my husband because he was dead set on killing me, because Luke and I were still lovers. So your baby will have a murderer for a father.'

'I don't believe you,' Fleur said flatly.

'That doesn't matter. Oh, he might be able to make sure he doesn't get called to account on this little princedom of his, but I'm damned sure Interpol will be really, really interested when I tell them what I know.' She whirled and left the way she'd come, her heels clacking along the terrace outside, as Fleur made a dash for the bathroom and was violently, horribly sick.

CHAPTER THIRTEEN

FLEUR was sitting on the edge of the bed when Luke came in. After one look at his dark, angry face she got unsteadily to her feet and said without preamble, 'Janna came. She said she's going to tell Interpol you murdered her husband.'

Heartbeats pounding in her ears, she watched him until he said in a voice that was completely matter-of-fact, 'Do you believe her?'

'Of course not,' she said, stunned. 'But she intends to make trouble for you. Why? I thought you were friends.'

'So did I.' He shrugged. 'I suspect she had me in mind for a second husband.'

Fleur suspected so, too, and she didn't know what to say.

Luke broke the taut silence with one word. 'No.'

'What?'

'No, I do not want to marry her, never have wanted to marry her.' His voice was utterly convincing. 'I'm married to you and I intend to stay that way. Relax—she won't go to Interpol. She knows I can prove I was nowhere near him when he went for that swim. I was sitting with the council of chiefs, working out what to do with him.'

Fleur should have been relieved. Instead, she said worriedly, 'Even if you can prove you didn't do it, the gossip and horrible publicity will tarnish your reputation—the world is full of people who'll say there's no smoke without fire.'

Coldly, lethally, he said, 'If she so much as breathes a word linking me with her husband's death, I'll slap a lawsuit on her that will strip her of all the money he left her in his will, however much that is.'

Janna didn't strike Fleur as anyone who saw much beyond her own needs and desires. She said quietly, 'Perhaps you should tell her that. She must have mistaken your kindness in giving her refuge for evidence of love.'

He looked at her with a twisted smile. 'There was nothing of love in our relationship,' he said. 'I've never loved anyone until I met you.'

At first Fleur didn't think she'd heard him correctly. When she realised he'd actually said the words, she couldn't bring herself to believe him. 'You don't have to say that.'

'I'm tired of holding it back,' he said laconically. 'I think I must have loved you when I first saw you. You were sleeping, white-faced and still, with your hair wild around your face, and then you opened your eyes and I saw that they were pure green, and I thought, *Hell! What's this?* I wanted you from that moment.'

Fleur yearned to accept the flat statement, but passionate desire was no substitute for the truth. 'No,' she said wearily, sadly. 'If you ever wanted me it was because I looked like Janna.'

'If I wanted you?' Luke stared at her as though she was mad. 'Of course I want you, you idiot! I still do. Do you think I can turn passion on and off like a tap?'

'Men can—'

He said something so rude she stopped and flushed, eyes enormous in her face.

'What do you know about men?' he demanded. 'Nothing! Yes, there's a basic level of crude desire that's easily aroused, but I'm no kid of eighteen at the mercy of his hormones. Couldn't you feel that when we made love? Hell, I had to exert every shred of control I had not to take you without thought or tenderness or anything but the hunger you rouse in me—'

Temper rising, she stared at him. 'You didn't have to,' she flashed. 'With all your experience, couldn't you tell that I wanted you so much that I wouldn't have cared if you'd flung me on my back on the bed and taken me without finesse? I only have to be in the same room as you to—'

Suddenly realising where this was going, she stopped, skin flooding with heat and colour.

Luke said dangerously, 'Go on.'

'No,' she muttered, looking away for an escape route. The very air seemed heavy, thick with potent, mindless emotion.

It was too late to get out of this with any dignity. Now Luke knew exactly what effect he had on her, and judging by the hunter's glitter in his eyes he was going to exact the most pleasure he could from her.

But he didn't move. 'It cuts both ways,' he said through his teeth. 'I haven't ever felt so helpless. I wanted you so much that I could taste it, and all the time you held back. Even when we'd made love, you wouldn't give me what I wanted.'

'What did you want?'

She held her breath. He hesitated, then said grimly, 'Do you remember that first ride we had— when we stopped to look down at the house and heard the *tikau* calling?'

Totally thrown by this, she nodded.

He said, 'It's a legendary bird, so shy that very few people ever hear it. When a man and a woman hear it together, the islanders believe they're lovers joined by destiny. My parents heard it. I'm not superstitious, but I think I knew then. I just wouldn't accept it.'

'But that was only the third or fourth day after we met—and you barely saw me for more than a couple of minutes night and morning each day—'

'I know. The whole idea made me angry. When I fell in love, I wanted it to be my decision, not because of some old tale. I knew I wanted you, but I didn't want to love so irrationally.' He gave a hard, humourless smile. 'I felt cheated of discovery, I suppose. Why are you shaking your head?'

'You couldn't have loved me then,' she said quietly, be-cause he was talking about lust, not love. 'You didn't know anything about me.'

He looked at her, and his eyes narrowed. 'By then I'd carried you to bed, so I knew how well you fitted in my arms. I knew you had a temper that went with your hair, that I wanted to kiss every inch of your exquisite skin, that when you smiled it did something that should be illegal to my mind and my heart and my body, and that you were intelligent and thoughtful and loyal.'

Flushing, she said, 'You couldn't have!'

'And that you blush charmingly,' he said with a wicked glint.

Her colour increased wildly. 'I can't help it.'

'I'm glad. I wonder if you'll still blush for me when we've been married forty years.' He came towards her, his intention plain in his hunter's smile. 'Of course I love you. I think of you incessantly and worry about you and want to chain you to my side. Hell, I dream about you, you red-headed witch. I plan to spend the rest of my life making you happy. If that's not love, it's close enough for me.'

Fleur's heart gave a great jump. Although she'd risked everything to marry him it had been worth facing the fear and prospect of pain and disillusion, because she loved him with everything she had.

Taking her hands, he said in a low voice, 'You asked me what I want. I want the same from you.'

'You have it,' she said, her heart in her voice, drowning in the dark grey of his gaze. 'You must know that. Completely and utterly and for ever. I think I started to fall in love with you when I opened my eyes and saw you looking down at me. Living here with you made me so happy, and as I got to know you I just fell all the way.'

In a raw, tense voice she'd never heard before, he said, 'If I'd had any idea that Janna was telling the truth about her husband I'd have sent you straight back to New Zealand the day we met. She was always a drama queen—I thought they'd quarrelled and she'd come here to teach him a lesson, make him jealous. I had no intention of letting her use me like that, so I immured her in a place where she'd be safe—and bored out of her skin. But he *had* beaten her, and he *was* obsessively jealous. And it turns out that the woman who died in very mysterious circumstances in his youth had been his lover, too.'

She shuddered, and he pulled her into his warmth and his strength, his arms clamping around her as though he'd never let her go.

The last of Fleur's defences crumbled into sawdust. Muffled against his chest, she wriggled until he loosened his grip enough for her to breathe.

He lifted her chin and said tersely, 'I hope she hasn't spoiled things for you—if I'd known that she'd come back spitting poison I'd have sent her on her way when she first contacted me.'

'And then felt responsible if her husband had killed her.' Fleur touched his cheek with a wondering hand. 'It must have been a horrible experience for her, poor thing. I think she's had a really bad fright, and to her you probably represent the sort of security that money can't buy. She's scared, and she knows that you would never hurt her.'

He said grimly, 'You're far more forgiving than I am. The Jannas of this world look out for themselves first, and as the widow of a very rich man she'll feel much better as soon as she gets her hands on the money. Do you still believe that I fell in love with you because you bear a transitory resemblance to her? Even though your hair and your eyes are natural and hers are fake?'

'What do you mean her eyes are—? Oh! Coloured contact lenses?'

'Indeed.' He kissed her eyelids closed. Breath warm across her forehead, he said, 'If you'd asked me three months ago whether or not I liked red hair I'd have said that I had no dislike for it. Now, because you have it, I love it. But, more than your hair and your huge green eyes and your magnificent skin, I love the woman I found so unexpectedly when I wasn't even looking. When you ran away I thought it was all over. Why did you go?'

'Because I thought you'd probably try to look after me in a kind, impersonal way, and I couldn't bear to have you as a friend or a benefactor when I loved you so desperately.' She sighed. 'I was terrified. I'm still terrified. I have this huge, all-encompassing love, and I just can't see how you can return it, because I'm not sophisticated or particularly clever or anything…'

He made a low growling noise in his throat and kissed the words from her mouth, and somehow she knew that everything was going to be all right, that miraculously she'd been gifted with what her mother had never known, once-in-a-lifetime love, the sort that lasted for ever.

When he finally released her it was with a little shake. 'You're everything I want. When you finally contacted me I hoped it was because you'd discovered—as I had—how wretched life was when we were apart. Then you said you were pregnant, and I realised that it was far more likely you were simply desperate. But I wasn't going to let you get away again. I forced our marriage, hoping that if I played my cards carefully you'd learn to love me.'

Her colour rose, because in his eyes she read the naked truth. But one thing niggled away at her radiant happiness. 'Do you still feel that that wretched little bird pre-empted things?'

He shrugged. 'Who cares? And I don't think I can allow you to call the hero of one of the best-loved and trusted legends in Fala'isi a "wretched little bird". I've accepted my fate—have you accepted yours?'

'Yes,' she said simply, and he laughed deep in his throat and lifted her high, and carried her across to the bed.

'Good,' he said, starting to divest her of her clothes. 'Now, I think we should seal our love, and then we can start talking about plans for a blessing for our marriage.'

Fala'isi was in carnival mood. Flower-decked islanders lined the streets, cheering and shouting, showering the big white wedding car with scented blooms. Tourists competed for the best sites, delighted at this unexpected extra to their holiday.

Smiling, Fleur waved until her arm was tired, then

turned to Luke's mother. 'I can't thank you enough for offering to come with me to the cathedral,' she said. 'I don't have many friends, and with no family I found myself lying awake one night wondering how we were going to fill my side of the church!'

'It's only a *little* cathedral,' Tamsyn told her comfortingly, taking her hand, 'and since we have more than enough relatives to fill the island I don't think you need worry. Dear girl, I only wish your own mother could have seen you looking so beautiful and so happy.' She blinked back tears. 'Darn, I don't dare mop these away, or I'll smudge my make-up! Fleur, we're delighted to have you as part of our family. I knew the moment I saw Luke with you that he's happier than he's ever been and as you positively glow, I know you feel the same.'

Fleur's smile was misty. 'You've all been so nice to me. I've never had a family before, so you must let me know if I do anything wrong.'

Tamsyn smiled. 'I can't see that happening—we love you already. Now, you'd better smile and wave some more, because we're nearly there and there's going to be a huge crowd waiting.'

Much later that night, after the ceremony in the flower-filled cathedral and a huge feast where she met even more Chapman relatives and most of the Fala'isians—or so it seemed—they were farewelled by song and dance. The exquisite singing of the islanders was still echoing in Fleur's ears as they drove back to the house.

'Tired?' Luke asked.

She said dreamily, 'In the nicest possible way. It's been the most wonderful day of my life.' She sat up straight as he guided the car onto the side of the road. 'Why are we stopping?'

But when he switched off the engine she heard it—clear, bell-like, the *tikau*'s song rang out in triumph through the steep green mountains and across the valleys.

'I thought we might hear it again here,' Luke said. 'Probably for the last time, according to Susi when she told me the legend again yesterday. Listening to her, I realised I'd forgotten one important part of it.' He smiled down at her. 'The bird doesn't cause people to be soul mates—it simply recognises those who are, and sings with joy at their happiness.'

The bird fell silent, and without talking they got back into the car again.

Fleur leaned across and kissed him. 'Something Susi told *me* when I was getting dressed this morning,' she said, her heart filled with such delight that there was no room for doubt, 'is that this baby is a girl, and the next three will be boys. What's her rate of accuracy?'

He laughed. 'I believe she's never wrong.' His wonderful voice deepened. 'Have you ever felt that there is nothing more in the world that you want, only to find out that there are still pleasures and challenges ahead?'

'Yes. Today. And every day since you told me you loved me.'

He held her hand beneath his on the wheel, and like that they drove down into the valley and into their life together.

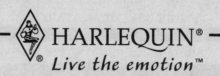

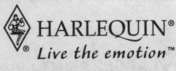

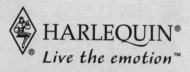

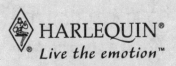

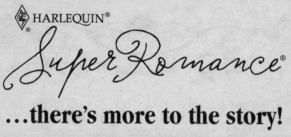

HARLEQUIN®
Super Romance®

…there's more to the story!

Superromance.
A *big* satisfying read about unforgettable
characters. Each month we offer *six* very different
stories that range from family drama to adventure
and mystery, from highly emotional stories to
romantic comedies—and much more! Stories
about people you'll believe in and care about.
Stories too compelling to put down.…

Our authors are among today's *best* romance
writers. You'll find familiar names and talented
newcomers. Many of them are award winners—
and you'll see why!

If you want the biggest and best
in romance fiction, you'll get it
from Superromance!

Exciting, Emotional, Unexpected…

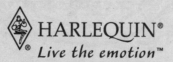

HARLEQUIN®
Live the emotion™

Harlequin® Historical
Historical Romantic Adventure!

*Imagine a time of chivalrous
knights and unconventional ladies,
roguish rakes and impetuous
heiresses, rugged cowboys
and spirited frontierswomen—
these rich and vivid tales will
capture your imagination!*

*Harlequin Historical . . .
they're too good to miss!*